run
farrukh dhondy

BLOOMSBURY

First published in Great Britain in 2002 by Bloomsbury Publishing Plc
38 Soho Square, London, W1D 3HB

A CIP catalogue record of this book is available from the British Library
ISBN 0 7475 5008 5

Printed in Great Britain by Clays Ltd, St Ives plc

10 9 8 7 6 5 4 3 2 1

This book is due for return on or before the last date shown below.

run

one

'I one Rashid Rashid, am dead. Dead and yet alive. Well, I must be alive if I'm writing this, because dead men tell no tales and this is a tale and it's straight up. Nothing underhand is afoot, as Herbert used to say. I know it's silly, like other things he invented, but I feel a bit guilty about him now. He comes into the story later. The last time I left him he was in trouble, but it's not good to give the game away so I'll tell you about him in another chapter because I've got to get there first.

I got that about being dead and yet alive from a book which I found in the library of this jail. I'm in jail, right? Inside. Away. Locked up. A cheater and a porridge-eater. But before you get excited, let me tell you I'm not a criminal. I'm not even accused of nothing except being foreign and I'm waiting for my case to come up and then they'll deport me. Maybe. To where? They don't know and I don't know and that's their problem till they do it and then it becomes my problem, because I'll maybe land up in a place which I don't know, and they may not have any Social or Sally or nothing, so I'll just have to tough up and see what goes down. Like Robinson Crusoe and Tuesday.

I told Kristina that I've got no people, no mum and dad, and she knew I was lying.

I'm fourteen years old and I'm writing this down to pass the time. Kristina says maybe she can sell it for me and I can have the dosh.

I said I'll write it like *Startrek*, not the same but like that, you know, a feller set adrift and having to come back and fight off all the evil that flies at you at the speed of light. Like this: 'Rashid Rashid making contact with base . . . do you read me base?' That's you, whoever you are. Say, 'Alpha the Romeo does the foxtrot' or stuff like that.

But then I found this book and it was true about being dead and yet alive – so I'll change the whole thing and get to the point.

There's not much to do here. Most of the geezers don't even understand English. They're all Romanian and Afghan and Kurdish and they probably can't understand a word on the telly because they switch on the comedy shows, right, and just sit and stare at them. They don't laugh. They laugh at the ads and wait for the football.

They're sad in here. Like some of them reckon they are Mafia, but if they were, then their mates would have come and got them out. Stands to reason. But they're still rotting in here, lining up in the corridors for the toilet in the morning and coughing to show they're in there because all the bolts are bust. So the Mafia theory is zapped, but still I stay away from those guys. One never knows.

If I have to be straight, most of them are probably illegal immigrants and the like. And they think I am one too. And I'm not. 'But the jury's out on that one, Ladles and Jellyspoons.' (That's Hervie the Pervie again.)

Kristina, the social worker, brought me here in a cop car. She told me it was just to find out a little more about me. She was putting me into detention and she kept saying she didn't want to, but they'd got an order out and she had to do as she was told by the Gestapo. It's outside London in the country, and it's no good trying to escape unless you want to walk in the fields because there's only one bus and the driver knows where you're coming from. Anyway, there's walls and the offices are on the ground floor and the rest of us are up on the other three floors so we can't jump out. Even though it's not a jail, we're locked up.

'I know you're British,' Kristina said, 'but there are no papers to prove it.'

She questioned me and she got well annoyed when I answered every question with 'dead'.

'Where's your dad?'

'Dead.'

'And your mother?'

'Dead.'

'Do you have any brothers or sisters? Any relatives?'

'Dead.'

'How would you like to go back to school?'

'Dead.'

'That's not very helpful, Rashid, so why are you doing it?'

'To get you dead annoyed,' I said.

It made her laugh. And that made me co-operate.

'Did you have any other names?'

'I did, when I was tiny, but I can't remember them. I think my dad's name was Rashid, so my mum just doubled it up. She didn't know many Muslim surnames and she didn't like the sound of the ones she knew, I guess.'

'I know, we checked with both your schools. We're only keeping you here because you ran away from the care hostel last time.'

'I'm at risk, innit?' I knew I was. Because the police, they'd taken Hervie the Pervie and they'd got Dr Bronco, whose real name was Gideon Das and some other things too. They'd tracked me and they'd ascertained.

'Right then, you say you're British, prove it,' I said to Kristina.

'I can too,' Kristina said. 'I've got papers! I've got a passport.'

'You coulda nicked it and stuck your own photo in it. Cheap. Four quid and the tube of glue.'

'Maybe. But I've got a birth certificate and I'm registered in a town hall in Wales.'

'So, I don't exist. You're trying to say I'm dead.'

'Don't be absurd. I'm trying to get you papers. Find out who exactly you are.'

'Thanks,' I said being well sarcastical, because it was cheeky her finding out who I was. Exactly and all.

'Look, I didn't mean to upset you,' Kristina said.

'I don't think you sussing this and that will do much good, because you'll have to look in the Bangladesh Town Hall. That's where I was born.'

'We are looking into that too. But you won't even tell me your father's name.'

'Shall I tell you why I won't tell? 'Cause I don't flipping know, do I? It was Rashid. My dad didn't want nothing to do with us. My mum says she was pregnant and she thought she could carry on with him – their relationship and that. So she borrowed some cash and caught a plane from Heathrow to Bangladesh, but he was already married there and had kids, so he said he didn't know my mum and she was just some white Jewish woman chancing it, trying it on. Imagine how that must have made her feel! You ever been through that?'

'No, no I haven't,' she said. It's easy to wind her up. 'But I can imagine. It must have felt awful. OK, so let's find your mum's birth certificate. You know her name. She was English. Where was she born? Did she have parents?'

'I don't mean to be funny or nothing, but she didn't use her real name. She's a dancer.'

'I thought you said she was dead.'

'She might as well be, she's gone off hasn't she?'

'Where to?'

'Not in this country. She used to go to Iraq and Israel and dance and she got thrown out of America. And one day she just went. Not long ago. Just a few weeks, about five.'

'And left you all alone?'

'She wouldn't do that. She wasn't a complete scab, man. Nah, with my granddad.'

'Now we're getting somewhere. So where is he?'

'Dead.'

'You've started that again.'

'No, he really is dead. And don't get all excited, because you're not getting anywhere. He wasn't my mum's dad, he was my dad's dad.' I could see she was getting well and unduly.

'Your dad's father was in this country? Why didn't you tell me that? When did he die?'

'Don't get unduly,' I said. 'One thing at a time. He was here, he was an illegal, and then he pegged it.'

I could see that Kristina couldn't ascertain.

'I'll write it all down for you, OK?'

12

She thought it was a good idea.

I said I had paper and that, and a dictionary and a thesaurus, so it wouldn't be pathetic. She said that was good. The workers love you to write things down. Like the police.

She was so well chuffed with my offer that when she looked at my feet and saw my grossly pathetic shoes with one small toe sticking out of the side she said, 'I'll get you some trainers. 'They've given me the money.'

'Not much they haven't and I don't want to wear bombers.'

'Bombers! Would I get you bombers? I'm sussed, man. I know where they sell top *Nike*, but cheap.'

'Thieved?'

'Of course not.'

She did get me them the next day. So I threw her a crumb, right. When she said, 'What was your mum's name?' again, I said, 'Not so much past tense, there. She's still alive, we decided, didn't we? Well her name is Esther. She called herself Esther Rabinovitch, but nobody else called her that. They called her Gypsy.'

'Why did they do that?'

'The earrings. She used to wear curtain rings instead of earrings in her ears, because we were too poor.'

She knew it was a wind-up and took it that that was all I wanted to say that day.

13

In the book from which I got the style of my story there's a man called Fabio Romani who is dead and still alive, because he gets buried and then he comes out, like still alive, not as a ghost or anything to get his vendetta, which is another word for revenge. He hates his wife and her boyfriend and he wants to come back from the grave and kill them. A woman wrote that book. Marie Corelli. Great.

I, me, one Rash Rash, I've got no one to kill, everyone's been good to me, man. But I am dead because I'm in this place – detention centre they call it. And I've been on the run so I can tell you some stories. Bad, wicked stuff some of it and some just what you'd expect and, then too, not exactly because they don't get it right on telly. I reckon the people who write stories for telly don't know chill from chillblains.

Have you ever seen a dead person up close? My granddad was my first. He was expired. And I saw it happening. In front of my very eyes. Untold horror, man. He choked. Choking and speaking at the same time. And I thought he'd come right out of it, but he fell down, just crumpled and he was nearly out but he wasn't dead. His eyes were open and frightened, like he'd seen something I couldn't see. And tears started bursting onto his cheeks. First I said, 'Just wait, I'll get some water,' and then I phoned the emergency, but they started asking me for names.

While I was calling I felt my granddad grabbing my

ankle and pulling me down, like a drowning man clutching at the grass on the bank. He rolled over on the floor and came to my feet and he pulled the phone wire. He was an illegal so he was scared.

I tried to get him to sit up and then I ran out of the flat on to the walkway to get help. I didn't know whose help. The neighbours didn't care for us and we didn't get along with them. The fellow next door and his wife didn't like me being half-caste because they thought Mum being white and all she should have married a Jewish fellow, and the people on the other side, all three families, were well nasty. Mum called one of their girls a low-life once and they just went off us since, cussing and blinding when they see any of us.

I knocked on the door of the black geezer who fixes Mum's washing machine, but he wasn't home. It was night and there wasn't no one about so I ran back into the flat and as soon as I saw him I knew he had passed.

I didn't cry and I didn't panic. I did love the old man, but he was a scrounger and he was drawing the Social on someone else's name, another Bangladeshi whose book and passport he had brought from Bangladesh. This fellow was lame or something, so granddad had drawn social and disability for years and every time he went to sign on he used to do this limp. He wasn't a good actor and he wouldn't have fooled me. I don't suppose he fooled the girls at the DSS either, but they thought it was less hassle to give him his cheque and move him on. He used to flirt with them to soften them up, tell them they were looking happy and that their faces were like lotus pads and rubbish like that, so they must have thought he was sad.

'Looking good today, darling, with lip like pomegranate,' he would say and they wouldn't even know what he was talking about.

You might think that having a dead person in the house is scary, but it wasn't. I left him be where he was on the floor, because I couldn't think who to call and I heard the telly which was still on and went and sat in front of it.

I wasn't really watching. I was thinking and slowly it kinda sunk in that he wouldn't be there when it was morning. Or the next day, or the next.

He used to wear a hat because someone in Bangladesh told him it was a good thing to do in Britain. It was a felt hat and the person who'd told him this thing had taught him how to touch it and say 'Good evening.'

He couldn't speak much English, Granddad, but he was a randy old bastard. When he first arrived I was only nine years old and Mum, who didn't expect him and didn't want him staying or anything, had to accept him and put up with him. He used to take me to school in the mornings and fetch me every afternoon. I was well embarrassed by him in his hat and his three old sweaters, one parrot green with yellow stripes, the other red, and a dirty grey one. He wore them one on top of the other with his Paki shirt sticking out from under them. It was well unstylish. Untold bad style.

I used to walk behind him to disown him but he didn't mind. He would pass bus stops and if a fit young woman was waiting for a bus, even if she had a baby, he was quite shameless, he used to tip his hat and say, 'Good evening. I invite you.'

The girl would just look away or tell him to drop dead. One of them slapped him once. A nasty smack, man, it left red finger marks on his cheek. Mum laughed when I told her. She laughed till she fell over and tears started coming down her cheeks. Granddad pretended he didn't know what she was on about, because he was pretending to read the Bangladesh newspaper, the same one he'd kept for months till it was grubby and the creases where he folded it were black, the pages stained with curry and tea.

After that time he became more careful. He picked up the caution, man.

He didn't know the operational motto, which I didn't know at the time either because Herv the Perv only taught it me later. It goes, 'If at first you don't succeed, forget it.' I find that of use. You live and learn to forego.

He told me his secret after a few months of living in our place. He'd wedged his way in. He turned up at our door and we were taken aback. Mum was well taken aback. He had a big suitcase and he put his arms around her and she didn't know who it was and must have thought that she was being raped or something because she started screaming and he said, 'Daughter, daughter, my daughter!'

Then she remembered that she'd met him once in Bangladesh when she went over to claim my dad's hand in marriage and he gave her the push.

'I am not your wretched daughter,' says Mum.

'I have come all the way from Bangladesh to very sorry you,' he says, pushing his bag through the doorway. 'Grandboy, you don't kissing Grandpapa?'

I wasn't, but he grabbed me.

'Don't worry, you are in good clutches,' he says.

'You can't stay here if that's what you're thinking, chum,' my mum says.

His face falls. 'Then I am hopeless.'

Mum put his bag out and was shutting the door behind him when he says, 'I am also fight with son. For you.'

I suppose he thought Mum would be grateful. But she was well annoyed and resistant.

When I went down to play I found him still in the

yard of the estate sitting on his case and he motioned to me but I paid no attention and went off to the park where we usually kicked a ball about. It was dark by the time I got back and he was still there. He called out to me. He didn't know my name. 'Grandboy!'

'The tramp wants you,' one of the lads said.

I ignored that, but when I went up I said to Mum, 'He's still out there.'

She knew straight off who.

'He is your granddad, whatever your dad says,' she said. It was bothering her that she had turned him away. It was bothering me and all.

'He's sitting on his suitcase.'

'Go and get him, the bastard,' she says.

Mum used to work at nights and come back early mornings when I'd be asleep. I never thought it strange being left on my own. I thought everyone was left on their own. She always told me not to open the door to anyone unless the place was on fire. I must have been all of eight years old.

When I got down to the yard, he had gone. I ran out of the estate past the other buildings on to the street and I spotted him. He was dragging his suit-case. I went up to him.

'Where are you going?' I didn't know whether to call him Granddad or not, because I didn't know how long Mum wanted to keep him and I just felt that it wouldn't do to get too friendly. You know, like they

19

say on telly, 'A dog's not just for Christmas', meaning that if you only want it for Christmas you shouldn't get too fond of it because you'll get depressed when you kick it out.

'I'll look some Bangladeshi peoples,' he said. 'One or two days I will find my villagers.' He took out a grubby notebook from his jacket pocket and started leafing through it.

'My mum says you should come to our house,' I said.

He couldn't believe his luck. 'That house?' he asks, pointing back.

'We've only got one,' I say, and then it hits him. He must have been worried, but he is crying now with happiness and he lifts his three sweaters and pulls the end of his shirt from under them to wipe his eyes, showing his rubbery, hairy belly to the world. He puts his hand over my head and mutters what I think is some spell. It was his prayers.

'Come on, come on, come on,' he says, walking ahead and leaving his wretched suitcase for me to carry. I drag it a few yards and he comes back and lifts it up on his shoulder. And that's how we get back with him leading me.

'A day or two, that's all, till you get on your feet,' Mum says and he shakes his head, like one of them toy dogs with loose necks in sockets, so I don't know whether he means yes or no.

* * *

He stays for ever. When Mum tries to raise the subject of his leaving, he just pretends he doesn't hear and stares at his Bangladesh newspaper.

He doesn't wander out of the house much. Not at first, as though he's afraid he'd get locked out when he comes back.

On the fifth night he is there, Mum's gone out to work in the West End where she dances and there's a knock at the door and a voice shouts, 'Sonny, it's the police.'

The very word gets Granddad going. He goes ape, man, runs around the flat looking for a bed to hide under. They knock again and I say, 'My mum said not to let anyone in.'

'You can look through the letterbox, son, we are the police. We believe you're in there alone. Has your mother gone off and left you home alone? It's breaking the law.'

I knew it was the old Bill. They talk funny so you can spot them. So that was it. The bleeders next door had grassed Mum up.

'I'm not alone,' I says. 'My granddad lives with us and he looks after me.'

'We'd like to speak to him,' the Bill says.

Granddad goes frantic. He motions with both hands to keep the door shut and puts his back to it. Then he says, 'Hullo, hullo, hullo, hullo, hullo,' and waits for a reaction.

'Hullo,' says one Bill. 'He does have an adult with him.'

Then the other one shouts, 'Can we have a word, sir?'

Granddad says, 'Granddad and Grandboy.'

'Some joker,' one of the cops says.

'No speaka-da-Ingliss,' says the other. 'OK, remind your mum when she gets back from whatever she's doing that Granddad better be there when she leaves you alone, because we'll be watching.'

Mum was pleased when I told her, but furious with the neighbours for setting the cops on us.

'Shall I let the tyres down on Hitler's banger?' I asked.

'Don't bother,' Mum said, 'I've got a better idea. When your granddad is saying his prayers, we'll open the door and let the sound out. Let them know that we've not only got half-castes, we've got a real ethnic minority here.' She chuckled. She thought that was dead revengeful.

'Hey, Granddad, why don't you sing some Bengali songs?'

'You want I should sing?' Granddad asked. 'I know plenty song.'

'Not now,' Mum says. 'Save it for when we're not here. Make sure you do now. Hitler and Eva next door, they're great fans of the Bengali hokey-cokey.'

'Hokey? What is hokey?' Granddad asks.

'If you don't know by now, don't mess with it. But really, Gramps, thanks for being here, saved my life. They'd have put me in jail. And you too, if you leave him alone, because I'm appointing you legal guardian. Not when you go out to work, mind you.'

This was a completely new idea to Granddad.

'We'll find you something. Work, dosh, money, pay the rent, pay for food, you know?'

Granddad shook his head. He pulled out a passport.

'I am taking rations,' he says, and Mum twigs that he's gone round the DSS with the help of some other Bangladeshis he's found through the mosque. He's signing on and saying he pays Mum rent.

He was a cunning old bird, my Granddad. He must have been to the mosque once or twice, but he gave it space too, because someone there may have recognised that he was not the geezer his passport said he was and that his name was different. And from what he told me, these blokes do blackmail on each other. Threaten to grass each other up unless they get paid a percentage. Which is good.

Each guy knows what the other's done wrong and he has that like a Damo Cleese sword on the other guy's neck. He can grass him up and gather. Or gather from the geezer himself for keeping stumm. You takes your choice. So when the guys at the mosque sussed him, he stopped bothering with them.

I sat up all night in front of the TV after he died – yeah, I might have dozed off, but I'd wake up and there'd be more ads for Gay phone lines and call the women of your dreams and stuff, and I'd turn over – and twice that night I went and checked him. He was dead and he was changing. His flesh had begun to relax and fall away and stretched his cheeks and made him look young even. And in the morning the place stinked, stanked, whatever. The dead body had crapped itself and there was yuckkk, liquid stuff all over, under him.

I didn't want to touch the mess and I was between crying and checking it out. I thought of the mosque. Religion deals with dead people, doesn't it? So I turn up and I say, 'I want to see your leader.'

It was a youth with a white cap who I saw first and I didn't mean to be cheeky or nothing, but I didn't know what else to say. The youth asked me what it was about and there being no harm in it, I told him it was about my dead granddad. He just nodded, like dead granddads were a part of everyday business and he took me to a massive fat bloke inside a pretty desperate room off a corridor in this mosque. He was the Herr Comptroller, like you see in the German videos.

His specs were thick, like the glass of goldfish bowls, and his belly was a whale. More than that, it was the ocean in which whales swim. It was figurative.

'All alone. Allah have mercy. I will send the boys. Now. They will go with you. It's good you come here. What's your name?'

'Rashid Rashid.'

'Double-barrelled, you will do the work of Allah! We'll bring the body here.'

He arranged it. The mosque was supreme.

Five guys came into the flat and took Granddad back and cleaned him up in the dead of night when no neighbours could have seen a body carried out. They kept chatting stuff to me, like Hindu and Urdu but it was all UHU to me, guy. I didn't know Granddad's real name, but I knew the name he had on the pass-port he was using to get his subs. So I gave them it and they said they were praying to Allah to accept this person with the following name into heaven. It wasn't his real name, so I guess the other geezer whose name and passport he was using is on the heaven guest list. Granddad's probably gone to hell. He deserved it a bit because in the little room next to the kitchen where Mum put his bunk, he used to keep his suitcase and he'd crammed it full of dirty pictures, magazines with serious and sundry goings-on.

The boy at the mosque, Ghulam, a flat-chested, thin fellow with a long head at the top of which he wore this white cloth cap, asked me if I had any money at home, because funerals cost cash. He said to ask my mum, so I informed him that she was away, abroad and not expected back. He said I should inform her of the 'events', which is what he called Granddad pegging it.

The man in charge of the mosque was a fat fellow called Abu Farid. He always wore a black waistcoat and baggy trousers like pyjamas tied with a string round his waist which he fiddled with and tightened every now and then. In my mind I called him the Mad Mullah from a cartoon I'd seen in a comic.

The funeral was crap. It started to drizzle and the mosque couldn't even spare four geezers to bury poor Granddad. They put him in a coffin paid for by the Social and the guy Ghulam started crying. He never even knew Granddad, never met him once, but he thought he oughta cry so he did and started beating his chest. If he'd beaten it any harder it would have caved in.

'What are you crying for? You didn't even know my granddad,' I said as they were piling the mud onto the coffin in the wet grave.

'You stupid boy, you have to cry at funerals,' Ghulam said. 'You have been spoiled by Britain.'

Abu the beard put his arm around me. 'We shall look after you till your mother comes back,' he said.

I couldn't tell him that I didn't know when my mum would be back. She had sent two postcards in the last month, from Israel and Beirut. Half of each of the wretched postcards was filled with paper kisses, big Xs. Sad. But it meant she had to write less. She never said much about where she was, except that she was dancing in clubs and living in hotels.

I had nothing to eat and no money when Granddad's Social stopped coming and I knew that if I went round to the DSS office and told them I was alone, they'd take me in. That's what happened to a kid in my class when his father moved him out. This kid is called Denzil and he has eight brothers and sisters and one day his dad says, 'There's too much people in the house,' and tells him to go. He's the old-est boy so they pack his bag and put him out and when his dad won't allow him back in, he gets taken in for social and psychiatric tests and then gets sent to a home. Which he said was great because there's breakfast and dinner every day and pocket money and they can smoke what they like and nobody tells them off. Except they lock the doors at ten or something and then you feel like you're in prison. Some of the kids beat the other kids and take their stuff off them. That's a real drawback.

Denzil was suffering, man. So for eight days I just ate what was in the house. There was nothing in the fridge. No one had been out to score provisions like, but my granddad used to make rice every day and he had a whole plastic bag of it, like a pillow with a zip and I boiled that and ate it with ketchup. I wiped out everything there was, cans of black beans and stuff that granddad used to buy from the smelly shop where they sold this wrinkled up dried fish and palaver. The place used to stink of death, man. The butchers who sold the meat at the back of the shop had aprons black with blood but the people that bought there didn't give a monkey's shake of the paw.

And when the food ran out I must admit I fell into shameful ways. I used to go down the lane, where there was a street market, after the barrows had all been packed up in their vans and taken home. There was always potatoes and onions lying around on the ground. Not just rotten ones, but stuff that had rolled off and stuff they were too lazy to pick up again. On any day you could pick up enough to fill half a carrier bag.

It was Abu the beard who caught me at this after the first few weeks. I was going to school and I never told no one what had happened at home, because they'd grass me and I'd get sent inside. Abu saw me lifting potatoes from the street and as soon as I saw him, I tried to pretend that I was just larking about, practising my bowling with the spare potatoes, but I think he must have watched me for a bit and seen me putting them in the bag because he comes up and calls me. He knows my name.

'You, boy. Rashid, you hungry boy? Your mother no come already?'

'Not yet,' I said.

'After evening prayers at mosque we are having a feast. You come,' he said.

I turned up. I was fed up of boiled spuds and if he'd sussed me begging potatoes, then I was already shamed up so I didn't mind scrounging.

I used to watch Granddad do his prayers so I knew what to do, but I hadn't bothered to memorise anything. I went through it, bowing and bending down as if I was looking in the carpet for Mum's contact lenses. I just moved my lips and said what the rest were saying. I used to do the same at school when they sang carols at Christmas which everyone except me, even the Paki kids, seemed to know.

The feast was good. There was hot milk and fry-up sticky sweets for after.

'How you living alone?' Abu the beard said.

I said it was fine but he wouldn't let it go. He said I must come and eat there the next day too.

The mosque wasn't a real one at all. It was just an old house on an ordinary London back street with a yard and an old converted horse shed in which Abu and other geezers used to live. In the evenings they'd have a council thing up there and Ghulam and six or eight lads would gather and Abu would talk to them after dinner. It was mostly stuff about how everything in the country was wicked. Abu reckoned there was someone who was putting all this wickedness about

29

and he mentioned Israel and I think was trying to get round to saying that everything wicked came from there – McDonald's, films, TV, Disney, computers, wine, women, music, you name it, he was against it. He had his knife into it. And of course anyone with any sense knows that McDonald's is American and Israel never invented TV or none of it.

I wasn't going to jump up and say, 'Hey, my mum's gone dancing in Israel, you know.' I kept stumm.

Now I don't know much about hypnotism. In fact to me, it's alien. But old Abu had these guys, the youth men who came every day and loitered, just where he wanted them.

'Mummy is not coming,' he said to me one day.

'I can't rightly say,' I told him.

'You are a good boy, but you need someone look after it, otherwise police will take it.'

I didn't twig what he was getting at just then, but it sounded like blackmail to me.

'The community is going to help it,' he said.

Sure enough, the wretched community turned up to help it. Two old guys came with their bags and bedding. They were both from the mosque. I had seen them before lying on the floor in the back room and scratching themselves. They didn't ring the bell or nothing. They had a key. The cheek of it.

I was watching telly and when I went up to them and remonstrated like, they pushed past me. They were both carrying torches for no good reason and they looked around the house with the torches and spoke to each other in their language and moved in, man.

I said, 'You can't stay here. What do you think you're doing? It's my mum's house.'

'Be quiet, I am getting headache,' one of them said, spreading his stuff out on Mum's bed. The other one had found Granddad's room and stationed himself.

I have to give it to Abu. It was a perfect scam. He knew I couldn't go to the police.

They slept there that night, and the next morning when I woke up one guy had gone out to buy stuff and he let himself in again. He had had an extra key cut and was well pleased with himself. The one he was handling was from Granddad's pocket which he'd looted. That's the kind of person. Looting the dead.

And then they started libertising, man, cooking food and pretending like they were doing me a favour in my own house. And they escalated their cheek, I tell you. They brought guests, other Pakistani men and asked me to turn off the telly while they were having a meeting.

I couldn't stand it no longer so I went ape. I took their stuff and threw it out of the door and shouted at them to get out. There were eight of them. Two of them held me down, looking puzzled as though I had no right to shout and demand their exits and another one went and fetched Abu the beard who came waddling in.

'What is the case?' he said.

'I'll tell you what the case is, mate. The case is you've moved illegally into my mum's house, and I'm sick of it.'

'Why are you troubled,' he says. 'We will pay the rent and I knows you. You needs mens for look after.'

'I don't need mens for look after,' I said.

'You do one thing, boy, you listen to me.'

It was the first time I'd seen him turn beastly. He meant it. And then he cooled off a bit.

'Mummy is beautiful Muslim woman. How will she say when she find that mosque is not look after the baby boy? That police is taking him away?'

Blackmail again. He was getting emphatic.

'Why you don't leave these people and come and stay with me in mosque?'

'I can't stay in your mosque,' I said. 'I can't even visit the mosque.'

I'd suddenly thought of a way to get shot of this shower. 'My mum would get very annoyed.'

'She will happy,' he said.

'No, she won't. She's Jewish.'

'What are you saying, boy?'

'I told you, my mum's Jewish. Her name is Esther Rabinovitch.'

'You are joking me.'

'No. Straight up.'

'And you?'

'If your mum's a Jew, you're a Jew.'

'And your grandpapa?'

He was now thinking that they'd buried him in the wrong place and the thought was spreading all over his face.

'Jewish,' I said. I was lying.

He was angry.

'Then why you come to us?'

'I had nowhere else to go. Everyone said Muslims are good Samaritans, they will help you out. I want to show you something.'

I went to Granddad's room and dragged his suitcase full of porno pictures out to the front room and opened it. I passed the pictures and magazines round.

Abu the beard was really shocked, blown away.

'This is blueprint,' he said. 'All bloody blueprint.'

He threw the magazines down on the carpet and the others, some of whom seemed quite interested in the pictures up to that point, also threw down the ones they were holding.

'But we've buried him in the Muslim ground.'

'I'm sure he won't mind,' I said.

One of the other guys said 'Jewish' and he gobbed on the carpet.

I wasn't standing for it.

'Oi, wipe that off, man. Have some manners.'

They just ignored me and started talking to each other in their language, but every now and again one of them would say 'Polees' and another would say 'Jewish'. So I knew they were talking about me.

'Now you can clear off,' I said. 'If it's all the same to you.'

Abu nodded his head.

'You are owing money for the funeral.'

'I don't owe it, my granddad does,' I said.

Abu nodded sadly. He wasn't stressed no more.

He gave an order to the others in Urdu and like robots they picked up their bundles and bags and stuff and cleared out.

Abu paced about the house thinking while they were doing it.

When they'd gone he said. 'Why is your name Rashid Rashid, if you are not Muslim?'

'It isn't,' I lied. 'It's something else.' I couldn't think what was a Jewish name for a moment, then I said, 'It's really Moses.'

'We have to make war to live in peace,' he said. I didn't know what he was on about, but he was depressed, man.

'Mummy not coming?' he asked.

I didn't say nothing. He took ten pounds out of his wallet. He didn't say nothing. He just gave it to me and then he left. I said he was depressed.

two

The invasion had left a lot of food behind. The guys hadn't moved their rice and lentils and joints of meat in the freezer and sacks of onions and potatoes. I was going to live like a hermit till my mum came back. But Abu grassed me, or one of the others did, 'cause the Social came round, a man and then a lady and asked me questions and turned up at school, and blew my cover.

The headmaster called me.

'Rashid, have you been living on your own?'

There was no point in lying. The headmaster has X-ray vision, as good as. He always knows when you're lying and he never lets go. Once he's on your case, man, he's there for ever. Everyone in school knew that.

'Till my mum comes back from holiday,' I said.

'I thought there was a grandfather in the case?'

I could have laughed when he said 'in the case' because poor old Granddad was in a wooden case, down in the wet ground.

'He took ill, sir,' I says. I wanted to break it to him

gently.

'Took ill? So where is he?'

'He died, sir.'

'How? What did you do?'

'Oh, the Muslim community took care of all that, sir. They were very caring and they were nursing him. He was very in with the Muslim community, sir.'

That was a good stroke, to say 'community'. That's the language these people understand. He seemed satisfied by that.

'And they send people to look after me, sir, like godfathers, sir.'

The head looked at the lady, because she was the one who'd brought the case from the Social. I mean you, Kristina, for whom I'm writing all this down. If you remember, that was when you set eyes on me. And I could see that you wanted to believe all this about the others taking care of me, but you didn't quite believe it.

Kristina shook her head. She wasn't buying it.

'We checked at the mosque. They said they don't know anything about him.'

'You must have got the wrong mosque. There are plenty of mosques,' I said.

'We got the right one,' she says.

'They must have moved the people on. You know, transferred them. They have a quick turnover them mosques.'

36

The head took his specs off and turned his X-ray eyes on me.

'You've been lying. Understandably. You must see we want to do what's best for you. You must tell Kristina how we can get in touch with your mother.'

That evening they were waiting for me after school and took me home, got my things and we moved to the care hostel on Lemon Grove.

The lemons were out for spring – like hell they were. It was a hole. They'd tried to make it nice but the kids had destroyed everything. The walls, the furniture, the carpets. It looked like every time they painted the wall some disturbed child put their tag on it. New carpet – cigarette holes. New furniture – penknife scratches. Toilet – clogged with cigarette packets, school books and other stuff that made you wonder how it got there.

Kristina showed me to my room. I was sharing with another kid who didn't stop crying all night. A sniveller. He was just as old as I was and he wouldn't say what was the matter, even though I asked him ten times. Then I respected his privacy like, and left him alone to rot.

Myself, I felt gutted too.

I missed my mum. It just came over me and kept coming. Suppose she'd written another postcard. I wouldn't see it if I was living here. And the bastards might close my flat down and give it back to the

Council or something. And suppose she was just round the corner, coming home. Maybe she'd got stuck somewhere abroad where there was no post so she couldn't write. She didn't even know that Granddad was dead.

I wrote about when he first came into our house and how she didn't want him. Well, later on she really did want him, even though she knew he was a bit of a rogue. He stayed four years and he learned to do the Christmas decorations and small things like that, which she appreciated. She couldn't stand the way he pissed all over the toilet and outside it and she shouted at him something rotten for that and for not taking his own stinky clothes down to the laundry in Socrates House, the next building from Plato which was ours.

I don't suppose she thought she was going to be long when she went away, but that used to happen to her. She once got taken on a cruise ship to dance and had to leave without picking up her toothbrush or nothing. She phoned to say she'd be away a few weeks and I was to tell Granddad and look after him and see that he washed his clothes. The last thing on her mind was that he would peg it.

And then a nasty thought struck me. Maybe she wasn't writing because . . . she was dead. I tried to push the thought back into the hole it had come from. But the thought slithered about my head, like an ugly smooth black monster in a lake and me trying to push it, will it, back underwater. I kept pushing it back and it kept powering to the surface. Till I said, yes OK, let's admit it then, play that game and suppose she is dead. Then all I got to do is ask myself what would happen to me.

So I ask myself and I can't give myself much of an answer, except that I'd grow up and then I'd do what I wanted to do. Maybe work. Get married and have my own wife and family. In my mind I couldn't see this wife and family, but I knew they'd be there and that was good and comforting. There'd be somebody, because somebody would want to marry me. Though I don't know, you may require a birth certificate to get properly married and I haven't got one.

Now you know what I look like, and that's not much and none of the girls at school or anywhere ever showed that they fancied me. I'm average. I got straight black hair and brown eyes and my voice is half on the crack. My mum sometimes calls me 'Billy Goat Gruff' because it sometimes comes out deep when I say 'Yes, Mum'. And I got big feet, but no belly or nothing like some flabby bastards.

I told myself it hadn't happened. My mum hadn't died. She was just a bit careless about time, like when she got deported from America and came back with jackets and jeans and clothes which were two sizes too small for me. Mums are not supposed to forget how big their kids are, but that's my mum – Esther Rabinovitch, dancer, the Gypsy.

She's actually stunning looking. You wouldn't think I was her kid, because my dad must have been dead ugly to supply them genes and chromosomes. She's got frizzy brown hair with a touch of red in it and she's well fit, even though one doesn't say that about one's mum.

She had a poster of her in a proper dance troupe, like, leading it. Not the kind of club circuit that she works in now. She is standing in front of some caravans and even though she's not smiling – no teeth or 'cheeeeez' – she is actually smiling with her eyes and the muscles of her cheeks are just about to pull into a smile. And she is the main dancer. There are others behind her but Mum's the star and the poster says GYPSY.

I knew a couple of her dancing friends, but they too were away. And I never knew whether she knew any men. She is dead fanciable, but I gather she was shy. Of me I mean.

She wouldn't bring her boyfriends back to our house because she was ashamed of it. Or maybe she didn't have any like she always pretended. I always knew she did, though. Especially when she took care to go out and dressed real fussy. Then she wasn't just going to see Sophie, her dancing mate, like she said.

She had good clothes, but just a few and she used to

make up and dress up real smart and that got on the neighbours' nerves and they called her a slag because they were dead jealous of her beauty and prospects.

Sometimes I thought maybe it wasn't the house she was ashamed of. Maybe it was me, like a mistake she'd made in her youth, like the girls you see on the telly who have babies when they are too immature, man. But I don't think she was shamed up by me because she always took me everywhere, except to work and when she went out some secret evenings with blokes and on her trips to Jersey and Paris and that. But always down the supermarket and into town and when she went swimming which was a lot. And she used to kiss me in public which was out of order and dead embarrassing when she done it in front of girls my age who would laugh and hoot. She's still quite young-looking, my mum, fresh around the eyes, like.

Sniveller, the boy in my room started getting on my tits. 'Little boys shouldn't have tits', my mum would have said to put me down. But he did depress me, man. He got me well wound up. I know it's cruel but after a while I didn't feel sorry for him, I just felt like thumping him and beating it out of him. Maybe it was because then he'd be forced to defend himself and if I saw some aggression coming out of this big bag of boob, it would alter my perception of him. But I resisted it. The head called me the next day from my class.

He came to fetch me at break himself and took me into his office and said he was just enquiring how I was doing in 'temporary barracks'.

I said I was fine. I hate complaining and I hate people who complain. Not just because it's soft, but because they don't think who they're complaining to and that the person can't do anything about it. It's like moaning about the weather. Nobody's in charge there.

The head said he was glad I had settled down and that I must tell him as soon as my mother made contact. I said I would. That was enough. He should have been able to figure out in his own dumb head that she wouldn't know where I was if I wasn't at home. But he was smarter than that.

'Of course she doesn't know where you've been moved to, but the Social Services will be on the look out for your mail and divert her phone calls. They should be on the ball.'

They were on a different ball from the Council who boarded up my house. They put large wooden boards across the door and the windows. I went and looked at it. They do that to stop burglars and rats and squatters getting in. So in a way it's good, but in my guts it felt like something final had happened.

While I was looking, the neighbour, Hitler's wife Eva, came in with her shopping. She got her keys and went into her flat and looked me up and down with her top lip clear of her teeth, like someone who's seen something disgusting. She was full of sympathy – not!

'And good riddance, I say,' she said.

'And how are little Hitler and little Quasimodo?' I asked, enquiring politely after her two brats. I coulda kicked her fat arse.

What did Herv the Perv used to say was his family motto?

'The intelligent must make concessions, dear boy.' That's how I felt after I controlled myself from kicking her. I forebore.

Then a guy comes to our Home, to Lemon Grove, from the telly. He is a producer, a white guy, and he's got this girl with him who says she's the researcher. The chief bozo of Lemon Grove, Frank, asks us all if we want to co-operate with the telly and that it's entirely up to us, and the kids all ask how much they're going to pay us. All the kids there, boys and girls are fully money-minded.

His girl then says they can't pay us anything because it's not legal and most of the kids lose interest. Then she says that they'll find ways of making us happy. They can pay expenses if we have any, like buying new clothes to be on the telly, or giving us the train fare to the place where we was born to help us remember things.

'I was born in New York,' one wise kid says.

'I was born on Concorde,' goes another.

43

Everyone starts getting interested again and Frank tells the producer that they can come back when they want and the girl says she can't promise that all of us will be on the telly, but she'll try her best. She is warning us that we may be only used for the research and not actually come on the screen because it's illegal to put the wrong kids on telly. I suppose the government don't want bad kids coming on and putting ideas into the heads of the good ones who may be watching in Wales or somewhere far away. That's why in adult TV you always get like bad people, but in kids TV you only get non-villainous kids who play the games and answer the questions and shout 'Yayyyyyyyyyy'. In Australian soaps and American cartoons you get some wicked kids. That's why people like them.

Of course, everyone in the Home wants to be a star, so they suck up to Delilah, the researcher girl who comes most days with a tape recorder and takes people away to talk to them.

When she says her name is Delilah, some smart kid says, 'I know – you were a hairdresser, weren't you?'

So she tells us that when she was born her mother had lice. There was an epidemic of lice in that hospital and so her mum had to be shaved clean so as not to get the lice on to the newborn baby's hair and so her father named her Delilah on account of her being responsible for balding-up her mum. It was a good story and she was telling us it just so we would get in

44

the mood to tell her our own stories. Sharp.

When she picked me out and we started talking, I quite liked her, you know. She was a young adult and she was slightly dark-skinned like me on account of being half from the West Indies and half from England, meaning her dad was black, but he was posh and a lawyer and so was her mum so she talked quite smart herself.

On the first day she was questioning me, I didn't twig what she was on about. She asked me my name and school and everything general like that to make friends without seeming nosy.

I made it all up. I didn't want to tell her about Granddad going dead on me, but she knew all about it. Frank must have told her.

The next day she goes on to Sniveller, who is still sniffing and wiping.

When she comes back to me, she starts by saying, 'Rashid, we're friends now. You must say what you want to say.'

I said sure I would, wondering when she'd mention some money again.

'I want you to think back to your early childhood.'

I nod.

'Did you always know that your mother was bringing in the money to the house?'

'I didn't know it, but I did know it was there. There was two of us and I wasn't bringing in the money. I didn't think about it – No, I tell a lie, I did.'

'Oh, did you?' she gets excited.

'When she used to leave me in the evenings with some child-minder from the next block, or leave me in Mrs McCartney's house to sleep, I started crying and protesting and she would say she had to go and earn the money to buy sweeties. That's what she used to say.'

'Did you know where she was going?'

'No. I was too young.'

'But as you grew up, did you ask, or did you find out?'

'Of course I did.'

'She didn't tell you herself?'

'I just knew.'

'You just knew? Can you remember a moment, like a particular day or an incident of any sort or a conversation in which you first realised?'

'I can't,' I said. 'But she would tell me about it and speak about the other girls. Some of them came home sometimes. Her mate Sophie.'

'She'd tell you about it?' Delilah seemed surprised.

'Sure.'

'What would she say? Can you recall that?'

'Of course. She'd tell me what she was doing, all the different things and numbers they asked her to do and how much she got paid and sometimes she'd moan about how mean they were and if she had friends round, they would join in and moan together.'

'And you had to listen to all this? When? A lot of the time?'

'No. We'd talk just normal. In the evenings. In the morning I'd get my own breakfast and go to school, because if Mum was in, she would be asleep, having been at work till late at night. That was after I stopped going to Mrs M's.'

'Rashid, did it ever disturb you?'

'No.'

'Was there ever a mystery about it?'

'No. She would show me how she did it. At home.'

Delilah was getting excited now but trying to show she was cool.

'By herself?'

'Sometimes with me. It was fun. That's how we used to have fun together, Mum and me.'

'Would you say that to the camera? If we disguised your face? You wouldn't have to demonstrate.'

'I couldn't demonstrate, like, alone. It would show me up.'

'I understand,' she said, going all serious.

I fancied this Delilah. I think she could see that. So I thought I'd take my chance. 'But I could teach you and we could like demonstrate in front of the cameras together.'

'I don't think that's a good idea, Rashid,' she said. 'But you can tell me what exactly your mum did, to demonstrate.'

'She's a professional. I can't dance like that.'

'What do you mean, dance?'

'She would put the CD on and dance and she would teach me to dance.'

'Yes, but what about her work. The demonstrations.'

'That *was* her work. That's what I've been telling you. She's a dancer.'

Delilah looked at me.

'Are you suddenly uncomfortable with this conversation, Rashid? We can stop and carry on later.'

'I'm fine,' I said.

'I thought you were. You are so matter of fact.'

'Why not?'

'I suppose there were no questions asked. You've told me something very valuable. Thank you, thank you, thank you. That's the nugget we were after. The nub of it. You see the producer started with the assumption that the kids get damaged through the process of discovery, about their mothers and other men . . . The boys and the girls, they fantasise about what their mother does with strange men . . . '

'There were no men. Just girls,' I interrupted her.

'What do you mean? There must have been men, but she didn't necessarily tell you. Am I right? She was just more up front about the lesbian aspects.'

'What are you on about? I was just saying there

were no men in the dance troupes. She danced her arse off and she was good.'

Delilah was staring at me. God, I should have caught on earlier. It hit me bull's-eye. Like an arrow through an apple on my head. Delilah thought my mum was a slag, a prossy.

'Hang on, what do you think my mum does?' I asked.

Delilah went dumbstruck

'She dances for a living. That's all she does. You got the wrong end of the stick, lady. You were thinking all this time that she shags for cash. Well you can stuff that!'

'We can talk about it later. Calm down. Maybe I went too fast.'

'Too fast? You're slow and slack, man.'

'I'm sorry. Maybe I asked too much. Now I've pushed you into denial.'

'My mum is not a slag!'

'I never used that word. It's sexist and unhelpful.'

'It's very helpful,' I said. I was well annoyed. 'You're a slag, a stupid slag too. She's a dancer and if you say one word against my mum, I'll smash that tape recorder and, and I'll get my mates from the mosque on to you. They hate the telly because they've met your type, nosing about and dumping on everyone . . . '

She panicked and left the room.

* * *

The next day she came back with another researcher, a man, and they whispered to each other when they saw me in the breakfast room, but they didn't want to talk to me no more and I didn't want to talk to them.

Frank called me and asked me why I had been rude to Delilah. I said it was because she was abusing my mum and he says, 'But that's what their research is about, about children whose mothers are on the game and when they begin to realise it and how they cope with it.'

'Well, my mum ain't on the game.'

'So you say,' he says.

I lost it. I saw red. I picked up my shreddies and stuck the bowl in his face and kicked him in the goolies with my trainers. I was shivering with anger and with fear. And it was my fear made me kick him in the face again as he went down. It was nasty, OK, but it wasn't that hard a kick and I didn't get him in the eye, just caught his shoulder with it.

You know in books they say 'something snapped'. I tell you, I know what that feels like, exactly. Something did bloody snap. My patience with this lot. It's like blood rushes out of your heart and blinds your brain with a curtain of red. It's like you're seeing a curtain of blood for a short second and you hit out.

The spilt breakfast made a mess, and poor Frank got doubled up and damaged.

I wasn't going back there. I wasn't going to school. I didn't have a coat, but I had all my dosh on me because in the Lemon Grove you didn't leave any of your precious stuff about. It would be gone without compensation.

I was on the run.

The only thought I had was that I had to find where my mum was. Now I wanted to see where she had worked. Where she said she was dancing. This bitch had put a worm into my brain and it was eating it.

I only knew a part of the name of the club she worked in, but I had a few quid so I took the underground and got off in Leicester Square and started looking for this club. I didn't know what street it was on. I knew it was called Fish something.

I walked about till it was getting dark. I walked down one street and up another, and then I asked some girls who were lounging about.

'Do you a know a club called something Fish and then something else?'

I felt stupid asking them, but they were kind.

'Do you mean fish and chips? Are you hungry?' one of them asked.

'No, I'm looking for my mum,' I blurted out.

'Why are you looking in Soho?' the girl asked.

'Because she's a dancer, she used to work here, but she's gone to Israel.'

'Haven't they all?' another one said and yawned.

'What was her name?' the kind one asked

'Gypsy,' I said.

'Yeah, she probably was a dancer. We wouldn't know. We're bad girls,' the kind one said. 'I hope to God you find her, kid. If you don't, come back to this corner and sooner or later one of us will turn up and we'll see you all right.'

I said thanks and pushed off. Then I came across it. It was a place called 'Neither Fish Nor Fowl'. I knew the name as soon as I read it. There was a girl at the door.

'I'm looking for my mum,' I said.

'How old are you?'

'I don't want to see the show. One of the dancers is my mum.'

She called a big black bloke from behind her and told him and he nodded.

'The dancers aren't in yet,' he said.

'I want to speak to the manager,' I said. 'She doesn't work here any more.'

'You speak Greek, then,' the black guy said, and they both laughed as they let me in.

The tables were empty and the place deserted and a geezer was handing some money out to two women who were wearing aprons.

He looked up from the table where he was counting his cash.

'Who is to letting you in? I will kick to them,' he said.

'My mum used to work here. I want to know where she went,' I replied.

'I knows you, boy. You is polees. Informationer. Please to get out or I kicks you.'

'I'm fourteen years old, for God's sake. I'm not a police informationer. My mother Gypsy, she used to dance here and then she got a contract.'

'No Gypsy here. Get vamoose before I kill to you.'

'She did work here,' I said, but the geezer was getting angry now and he stood up. He was going to hit me.

'You are childers. I can never beat to you. Just go.'

'She was called Gypsy. Esther.'

'My son, I bleed to you, but I don't know for nothing anythings. Go in outside street.'

I could see he didn't know the name. I went in outside street.

On the way back I saw the street girls again.

'Find your mum?' the kind one asked.

I said I hadn't.

'She'll come back. If you need us, we're here. You got cash?' she said.

'Oh yeah, I live with my granddad,' I said.

She waved goodbye. I couldn't have taken money from her. But I haven't forgotten her. She didn't even know me.

three

There was nowhere to go. I thought of going to Israel, so I went to a newsagents shop which kept books and things, A to Z kind of books, and looked at the shelves. There were maps of Britain and London, but no map of Israel.

'Do you have a map of Israel?' I asked the old Asian bloke behind the counter. He had nothing to do because there was no one else in the shop, so he came out and started looking at the shelves. He didn't know what he had in his own shop. Then he pulls out a book called 'Road Map of Europe' and says he'll soon find it.

'This is the book you want,' he says with great confidence and goes behind the counter and starts leafing through it.

'Very funny, no Israel,' he says.

A white bloke comes in wanting to buy fags and he hangs about the counter while my man is going through the thick map book for the third time.

'Sorry, stupid book. They are not listing Israel,' he says and carries on looking, ignoring the bloke who's come in for the fags.

'That's because it's a book of European road maps, Patel,' the white bloke says.

'I know what it is,' says Patel, 'I have found the flaws and will complain and make a million pounds.' He snaps the map book shut and hands the bloke a packet of fags. He knows his brand. The bloke gives him the money.

'I don't think you will, Patel, because Israel is not in Europe, see? It's in the Middle East.'

Mr Patel thinks this is funny and appeals to me.

'You see these fellows?' Mr Patel leans menacingly over the counter. 'My dear chap, I saw Israel in Eurovision song contest last week.'

'I keep telling you, Patel, don't believe everything you see on the box,' the bloke says and leaves with a laugh.

'Sorry, no map of Israel,' says Mr Patel.

It was a stupid idea anyway. I thought I'd check the main cities and maybe get there and then check every club in the city. That way I'd find her.

But I didn't have the dosh to buy an air ticket and anyway I didn't have a passport and one of the kids at the hostel told me that you have to have papers to get a passport. You have to have relatives and family. They don't give passports to kids without family.

That was when I started thinking hard about my

family, my mum's folks. She didn't come from nowhere. She had to have a dad and a mum, though I knew she didn't have brothers or sisters, or I don't think she did. She told me that my grandma was dead. But she never mentioned her dad, my other granddad. I couldn't recollect her saying that he was dead.

I walked back to our flats from Soho and that took me all of an hour. I get to our gallery on the third floor and the first thing I see is that the wood on the front window has been loosened up by tramps or kids or crack-heads or whoever, and when you pull, it bends back. The glass of the window behind it has been smashed and the window opened up so you can climb in.

I look around. There's no one in the yard, so I pull the thing back and help myself in. It's funny breaking into your own house. It's dark in there because everything has been boarded up. I feel my way to the kitchen. I can walk about in the dark in that flat. I know where Mum keeps candles. The kitchen has light from the window because they haven't bothered to board up the back. I get the candle and go to the gas to light it but the gas and the clicking spark that lights it have both been turned off. I get to my bedroom which is also at the back of the flat and has some light in it.

My room was in a bad way. Whoever got in had smashed everything. Pulled my wardrobe door off so it was left hanging, smashed the wooden sides of the bed, thrown the mattress on the floor and taken off all the sheets. It was chaos. They had ransacked my chest of drawers and smashed the drawers up, maybe for lighting fires. Next to the mattress there were empty milk bottles, some broken and cigarette stubs every-where and a little envelope thing of matches from a posh hotel.

I lit the candle and looked around the front room. It was also bashed in. Nothing was left as it was. The telly was gone and the CD player. Mum's books were torn and thrown about. It looked as though someone desperate had been looking for something. The sofa was turned upside-down and the cloth at the bottom ripped.

The sight of my own home like this gripped me with fear. Everything we'd like built up, so easily just torn and dumped. I went into Mum's room. Her clothes were all scattered over the room and above her wardrobe there was an old hat box which the destroyers had dumped on the floor. I had looked in there just once. It was where Mum kept her junk.

It was junk. There was the statue of a clown, made of wood. An antique one with its paint flaking. Behind the paint on the clown's face there was something that stopped me and made me look again. Usually, see, a clown is just a clown. Every clown looks like a clown, like the job he's doing, but this one, this statue, had the face of an actual person because the face had muscles and wrinkles and you could see that it was a man doing the job of a clown. A real man with a real face who could have been doing something else.

The statue of the clown had a polka-dotted red umbrella, folded and resting on the ground like a walking stick. Except that the folds of the umbrella were like a little cone basket. The paint, red with green and black dots, was nearly all gone, but the wavy surface of the folded umbrella formed a little pocket and in the pocket was a yellow bit of paper.

I unfolded it and could see that it was nearly cracked where it was folded. It was a note:

For Josh,
Be luckier than old Stanislav.
My face, my life, my sorrow.

I folded the note and tucked it back in the umbrella.

Who was Josh and who was Stanislav?

I looked back into the hat box. There was a dumb-bell, a metal thing with scratches of names all over it. The names were still clear, scratched by nails or dia-monds, maybe. There were thirty names. 'Alfonso, Alfred, Binny, Betty . . . ' all the way down the alpha-bet to three Zs – 'Zeno, Zak and Zaza'.

Squashed beneath the dumbbell I found a feather boa, some old carved chess pieces, a little cloth bag of yellowing powder, a large metal ring with an American Indian's head on it, an animal's tooth in the velvet of a jewellery box, a little plastic plaque which said 'Josh Rabbit' and below that on a scroll the words 'Tiger and Lamb'.

And who was Josh Rabbit?

I took the clown and its note, the dumbbell, even though it was heavy, the animal tooth and the plastic plaque. I put them in the bag with my shirt and underwear and thesaurus and dictionary and quit my flat. Was I sad?

Yeah, I was sad.

I got out the way I came in and some kids playing on the gallery looked at me and shouted, 'Beware, tramps!'

I wanted to go in the direction opposite to school and the other way from Lemon Squeezy so I hopped on a bus which went to a garage up north.

But where was I going? It hadn't taken me, like ages to work out what I wanted to do. It came to me in a flash, like seeing how the last piece of a jigsaw fits.

Sometimes I can't remember whether I dreamt something or whether it was true and actually happened. And there are things which I think I know which are half and half. I feel they actually happened and that they were made up by my imagination. Stuff I had conceived.

Like the story of my grandfather, my mum's dad. Did she tell me about it when I was a kid? I think I can see her giving me a bath, bending over the tub and shampooing my hair and washing it off with the shower and the shampoo stinging my eyes even though I scrunched them up tight, and she's telling me this story to shut me up and stop my protests. The story was about how she was born in the English Channel on board a ship because her father was a strong man in a circus. Or had I seen photographs of him in a lion skin, a bald, scary bloke lifting a platform with a horse on it. The horse must have been terrified to have this geezer get under it and hoist it up.

I don't know if that was half a dream. What I do recall is that, yeah, my mum was born on the water. I remember that because she said if you were born on a ship and you weren't in any country, then you could be a citizen of the place which owned the ship. I think she said it was Egyptian. She was born on an Egyptian ship and could be an Egyptian if she wanted.

And the other thing I remember was that I asked her where her father was and whether he was dead. This was after Granddad, my Bangladeshi granddad moved in on us. She didn't tell me much. She shook her head. So he wasn't dead. I began to calculate, like. My mum isn't that young. You'd think that if she was a dancer she would be sixteen years old or something, but she had me when she was only eighteen and so she must be well thirty-two and that would make her dad maybe fifty-two or maybe sixty-two or even seventy-two.

Where do strong men from circuses go? Do they change jobs when they get old? Do they hold the horses while other strong men lift them up? Do they retire to a home for strong men from circuses, who are tired of being strong and have become weak?

If I could find this grandfather – not the dead one which I'd buried – then I'd have some family in this country. Maybe he had other kids. I didn't fancy going to Egypt and telling them that my mother was born on one of their ships and could I stay. Yes, I thought of going to Bangladesh and looking for my real dad, but how would I get there without a passport, and smuggling myself was out. I had seen on the telly that three asylum seekers who got into the luggage box of a plane by hiding in suitcases had died of cold because it's freezing in there. That's well desperate. And sad, man.

I said 'last stop' to the driver and he asked if it was half fare or what. I paid and went upstairs. I was waiting for a cop car to come alongside and stop the bus and drag me off it and charge me with assaulting Frankie, kicking him while he was down. That is Common Assault, and if his face was cut and bleeding it would be Actual Bodily Harm, only I was too young to go to jail so they'd send me to juvenile detention. A kid like me, respectable, not low life and thieving and that. I never done none of those things in my life though I knew plenty kids who couldn't live without being bent in some way – nicking things, vandalising stuff, mugging, breaking into cars, anything. My mum hadn't brought me up like that and now this cow Frankie had her down as a prossy.

Maybe they'd written it in the registers they kept on kids. And the shame of it was they were going to put me on the box talking against my mum.

Which made me feel sorry for Sniveller, because he was talking to Delilah. She was in with him every day. Maybe his mum really was a prostitute. Or worse still, she wasn't, she was just a dinner lady and they were making him say she was a slag for sale. Other kids too. Maybe that whole Lemon Squash was for the kids of mums who were on the game and I'd got put there by mistake.

I couldn't say I hadn't done it, kicked Frankie, but then it was sort of self-defence and Delilah had started it all because she thought she was really 'street' because her dad was a posh, black lawyer.

When I thought again about her face when I told her that I'd get the lads at the mosque on to her, I had to smile. She'd got a bit nervous of that. It well shivered her timbers.

I got off at the last stop. I was the last person on the bus and the driver watched me as though I was up to no good. He'd clocked me all right and if they ever put out an ad for me on telly, or in the papers, he'd be the first to grass me up and slobber about with his tongue hanging out for a reward. Weasel with biceps! He looked like one of them know-alls who grass people up and then go to the pub and tell their mates, 'Yeah, it was me, right, got the ABH kid. Single-handed – flash about, flash about.'

That kind of person makes me sick. But still, he was the only one around so I had to ask him.

'I am looking for a circus,' I said.

'Get lost,' he said. 'Get off out of my bus.'

That was that. He didn't know any circuses was what I concluded.

I didn't know where I'd got to. I looked about me. From the top of the bus all the way I looked for the large commons because that's where the circuses would camp. I reckoned that if I found one, I could find the next one. The circus people probably knew about each other and just by luck they might have heard of my grandfather or maybe I looked like him. If he was called Rabbit, that wouldn't be hard to trace. It flashed through my mind that I could look him up in the phone book, but then he wouldn't have settled down and got himself a phone in London, would he? Or my mum would have known about it.

It was still London where I was, but I forget the whole name of the place. It was called somebody's 'End' and I remember that because it's like calling a place after somebody's backside – Aylmer's End or something. Where Aylmer dropped dead.

There were houses and fields and then a high street with shops. A light-goods truck stops outside a pet shop as I'm walking past and the driver steps out and opens the back. There's no one else on the street except a few old ladies. In the back of this truck is a stack of wood and wire cages. The driver goes to the back of the truck and starts heaving them. He pulls one way and the other. He gets one right to the edge and I'm watching him. He's not going to make it. If he pulls that cage down, it'll crash and maybe knock a bit off the new wood and ruin it. If he lets it go, it'll topple the ones on top of it. He is well and truly stuck. He looks round at me looking at him, so I think of moving on, accepting that I won't see how this one ends.

'Oi, kid, I'll give you a couple of quid if you help me unload these. Come on, get on the truck and grab the ones on the top.'

I took employment. I jumped on the truck and he jerked the bottom cage loose and then he asked me to hold his end while he got the heavy bit off the lorry. Together we carried this square of wood and net, a box without a bottom really, to the side alley next to the pet shop and through to the back yard. We unloaded the rest in the next hour and, true to his word, he gave me two quid.

He said he'd give me another two quid if I helped clean up the shop. We went in the back way and he opened it up for customers. The place stank. It was deadly, but he'd got used to it so he didn't notice the pong. I couldn't breathe. Definitely not worth two quid. I said I had a previous engagement.

'OK then. Thanks for helping with those.'

'What are they?' I asked, knowing they were some kind of cages.

'They are rabbit runs,' he says.

'But you put the rabbits in there to stop them running?'

'Right,' he says.

'It should be called a 'Rabbit Can't-Run'', I says.

'And you should be called a smart-arse,' he says. 'Do you live around here. You can come again and muck out for me.'

'No, no, I'm not from round here,' and then, in case he became interrogative, I started in on him. 'Do you do big animals too?'

'What do you mean, crocodiles?'

'No, rare pets, like wild things.'

'Strictly domestics. We go to snakes, but no further than that.'

'I've only seen snakes in the circus,' I said. It struck

me that I could turn this talk my way.

'I used to supply snakes regular,' he said. 'All imported. There aren't any big snakes in Britain. Only little ones. Grass snakes and adders.'

'Did you supply them to the circuses?'

'Don't keep on about circuses,' he says. 'Snakes don't go in circuses. Anyway, shouldn't you be in school?'

'School? How old do you think I am? I left school when I was sixteen. I'm a midget. That's why I'm looking for a circus,' I said, but I knew he was going to be shirty about this so I began to push off.

I couldn't get that out of my head. A 'run' is something with which they stop you from running.

The rabbits would get all excited when they thought they were being put in a 'run' and then the wire and walls would close in. This side, that side, every side. And they'd know they'd been had. No rabbit, no run.

And my grandfather must have been called Josh Rabbit. That's who the note was written to, and the name on the plastic plaque. So I could be called Rashid Rabbit if I took on his name.

I got some distance from the pet shop and tried to figure out what I was doing and where I was going. I had been given the word: run. I was on the run. Frankie, the police, the head, Kristina, all were after me. What it is to be wanted, man!

I had to leave London.

At the end of the High Street there was a bridge and across the bridge was the railway station. It had a different name from where the bus said it had taken me, but I let that pass. I went on to the platform. It was well into the afternoon by then and the platform was deserted except for a young man who was, like, the official there. He had his railwayman's cap pushed back on his head and huge bulging eyes like snooker balls. Toad's eyes really under sad lids.

'Where are you going, sonny?'

'Where can I go for a quid.'

I was thinking I'd save the rest of the two pounds I'd earned for a burger at Macky D's.

'For one twenty, on a half fare, you can get to Slough. Is that where you want to go?'

'I was hoping you'd say that,' I said. 'It's where I want to go.'

'No you don't. You've never heard of Slough. Can you spell it?'

'Don't be silly. Of course I can spell it.'

'You running away from home then?' he asked.

I didn't answer.

'I don't blame you,' he said. 'Go and join the Navy. That's what I wanted to do but I ended up on the railways. My eyes, I got these bulging eyes. They refused me. My dad said, 'ships, railways, it's all transport, innit?' and I suppose he was right.'

'I thought I'd join the circus,' I said.

'Then you're headed the right way. They leave London as it gets to winter and go outwards. Then in late spring they come back, like asteroids caught up in a planet's gravitational force.'

The guy was crazy.

'Actually, Slough is where my grandma lives and I'm going to see her,' I said, because I didn't want him to get suspicious and ring the police after I'd left.

He was dead good because he said, 'That's disappointing. I thought you were really going to join a circus. Any rate, the ticket office is shut, but you can say you thought you'd pay on the train.' He winked at me with his big frog eyes.

I was the only person who got on the train when it arrived and the station man spoke to the driver who was also the conductor. Maybe he did magic too and sang songs to entertain the passengers. He was an Asian bloke with a turban.

'Give my regards to your grandma,' says toad-eyes as he waved the train off. 'Is she young and pretty?'

'She's got big la-las and no morals,' I said.

He laughed loud.

'Did you hear that one? Kuldeep Singh? Did you hear it? Give the boy a free ride. And don't you give your grandma no grief now, boy.'

He was still laughing as the train pushed off.

Kuldeep Singh came to where I was sitting. He must have put the train on automatic pilot or something.

'Albert loved your joke. He's going to laugh himself sick.'

'It wasn't that funny,' I said. 'And I don't have a grandmum.'

'Oh it was funny,' said, Kuldeep Singh. 'It's the combination between the things you said. That's where the joke is.' He didn't take the money for the ticket. Though he did give me a ticket, a scrap of paper, in case the inspector came on board, he said.

'So what happened to your grandma?'

'Nothing, I never had one. Not in Slough. I don't even know where Slough is.'

'It's a wonderful city,' he said. 'Your grandma with the big things, she should relocate.' He grinned. Then he got a bit serious.

'So, why are you going there anyway?'

'As good a place as any.'

'Are you in some trouble? You are an Asian boy, aren't you? What's your name?'

I told him.

'Muslim,' he said. Now he looked worried.

'Where are you staying in Slough?'

'I don't know.'

'Look, I want to help you. I won't tell the police or nothing. Lot of people, girls, boys, who run away pass

69

through here. I talk to them sometimes. You are not running away?'

'No. Nothing like that. I just need to stay away from London for a week or two. My stepfather is a sailor and he's in town and he beats me. In two weeks his ship will sail for Venezuela and then I can go back to Mum.'

I didn't even know if ships could go to Venezuela, but it was the first thing that came into my head.

'I understand,' he said. 'Sailors are rough. Albert wanted to be a sailor but they wouldn't take him because he has bulging eyes. Did you notice?'

I said I had noticed.

He had a belt with an old-fashioned ticket pad on it, but it had a little computer machine inside. He walked off now to drive the train and I could see him beyond his cabin door fiddling with the controls and on the phone.

Then he came back.

'You want to live in Slough, I can fix for you.'

I looked into his eyes. He was being kind and no tricks.

'Go outside the station to taxi rank. Don't wait in queue. I will tell my friend Das to pick you up and take you to his house.'

'I've not got much cash,' I said.

'No, no, no no. No money. Rashid, you are an Asian boy. You have a little problem. We were once

70

Asian boys. Das and me. You know how long we've known each other? Twenty-two years. We were Asian boys, also. Always having some problem. We can help each other. We can help you.'

I had never heard stuff like that before, but he was convincing when he said it.

'I mean, it would be taking liberties to land up at his house.'

'Not if he takes you himself. He drives a cab. He does business. You will be safe.'

'Thanks,' I said.

'We are arriving,' he said and went into the cabin again and made his call.

It was a sunny afternoon in Slough and there was no one at the cab rank except Das who drove up when he saw me.

'Hey, respeck! Kuldeep phoned on the cell and said you was here. Nice,' he says, opening the cab door for me. I got in.

'No luggage. Travellin' light. I just cain't wait to be with mah baby tonight. Rashid, Rashid, Rashid.'

'Thanks for picking me up,' I said

'Cool, cool, cool. You beating the system. I'm against the system. Let's beat it systematically.'

I didn't know what he was saying. He was weird. He was wearing dark glasses and had his hair in rasta locks and I knew who he was immediately.

'I've seen you,' I said. 'On the telly.'

'Yeah maan, I am a star,' he smiled.

He pulled off his shades. It was him. Asian bloke.

'You saw the programme then? I mashed it up, maan.'

He grinned.

I had seen the programme. In the house in Lemon Grove. All the kids had watched it. It was on Channel 5 and it was wicked. About these black guys, Asian guys and white guys all trying to cut each other's throats for taxi fares, having punch-ups outside clubs and trying to bump each other's cars when they met up in the streets like dodgems, but with real cars.

'Did you see that chase, man?' he asked proudly.

'Yeah, that was the main scene, man,' I said. 'I loved it. I was going to write to you and say to keep it up.'

'Yeah, yeah, yeah. Matter of fact some girls traced me and rang me after the programme. Well blissful. The price of fame.'

In this programme he was there driving one of the dodgem cars and he bashed his car at speed into the side of another geezer and then bounced off and drove away and beat the other car what was following him. They got it all on camera.

'Some of the kids in our home said it was set up. But I know it wasn't. Was it?' I asked.

'Set up? The bastards nearly killed me,' he said.

Then he was shown once or twice again arguing

with the enemies and I remembered him clearly. So wow, I couldn't believe it. I'd landed up with the man himself and now he was going to be a friend of mine.

Das was wearing a rasta cap, not red, green and yellow, but like blue and black or something. He had one gold tooth and a wicked grin and even now he started driving like a maniac. His cab had a heavy smell of perfume.

I stared at him. He grinned back.

'What's the matter, Rasheeeed. Never seen a Blackistani before?'

'Not a grown-up one,' I said, and he thought that was desperately funny.

'Kuldeep tells me you slaughtered one of his railway brethren wid a joke. Keep them coming. Do you know this place. Marlboro Country. Sleepy hollow?'

'I never been here,' I said. 'But it can't be sleepy with all those car chases and rumpus, man.'

'That's not every day. But you saw what I predicted on the telly, man. This thing here, these taxi wars gonna lead to somebody getting killed unless the brothers see sense and give up violence.'

All the time he was driving he had his mobile phone switched on to a thing which spoke to him on a loudspeaker and he could talk back in it. Guys phoned him up, one every twenty seconds. They just left their names because he didn't reply, just nodded when he heard their voices and repeated their names.

'This is Percy, calling Doctor Bronco.'

'Dolores. Doctor, I need treatment. Call back.'

'The Gaylords, Bronco, Doctor sahib. Never get you, always have to speak to the machine.'

He was delighted with all the messages as they came and he would mutter to himself, 'Percy, Dolores, Gaylords, right, right, right.'

He switched the phone off after we left the town centre. Then he suddenly reached for his belt as he was driving and pulled a small pink plastic water-pistol out of his belt. He pointed it out of the window and said, 'Ping, ping, ping, ping, ping, dhishoom dhishoom.'

Then he rolled the window back down and carried on driving, putting the pistol on the dashboard.

He looked at me.

'There are taxi wars in Slough. I just eliminated two taxis from the rival firm. Everyone's fighting everyone. You chose the right town. Every maan try and run every next maan outta town.'

'But you don't use real guns?'

'I don't. I and I is peace-loving and respeckful of life and Jah's creatures and their cattle,' he says.

Das is a miracle. I like the way he talks, the way he is cool.

'I am by birth a Bengali, but you know what mek me dis way? Consideration.' He taps his head to demonstrate thinking.

He takes me to his place which is a quiet house, not on an estate but in the street, like. His own house. It's different from the flats in which people live. It's much more like you see on the telly, with a hall and stairs up and the kitchen at the back and the telly room in the front and plenty of rooms, mostly empty, with no furniture even.

Das gives me a room to myself and he says he's got to go back to driving but I can play with his computer or watch telly. Or go out and come back at seven when he'll be back. He can get me keys next day.

I say I'll stay. I didn't want to tell him that I was looking for a circus. I'd tell him later when I'd won his trust, otherwise he'd kick me in the street thinking I was a lunatic. The fact is I have nowhere to go in Slough and I'm scared that if I come back at seven and I don't have a key he won't be here and maybe he'll have changed his mind or something.

The only thing he told me not to use was the answer machine on the phone. He went off and I could hear the messages coming through. Like his mobile, they were all for Dr Bronco and Das had told me that that was the name people used for him. He said the English couldn't pronounce Das, it was too difficult for them, so they called him Dr Bronco. Besides he didn't want to tell everyone that it didn't rhyme with 'gas', but with 'arse'. That shamed him up when he was young because a cruel teacher told him he must say that every time he was asked his name. So he stuck to Dr Bronco. Oh yeah!

He was in and out of the house.

'You is my younger brother. 'Nuff respeck,' Das said.

I knew this kind of talk. There were black guys in school who used to do it to be hard, but Bronco was doing it because he didn't like being Indian and rhyming with 'arse', or that's what I thought at first. Wrong again, Rash!

He gave me great food and he opened a lot of cans of beer and I don't drink so I just drank juice and that, but he was great to me.

And he could read my mind, because after he'd had about eight beers, he was still driving his cab out. He must have been well drunk, but he kept going off for half an hour at a time, right through the night and he left me watching telly and he'd come back and have another drink and tell me to go to sleep.

Then he says, 'Rashid, I don't play Dr Bronco to be hard, you know. I'm not ashamed of being Asian or nothing. I'm proud of it. But my mates they all got me into it and then I started a business and it was best to be Dr Bronco. So don't get uncomfortable, OK? To you, I'm just Das, big brother Das.'

He took his shades off then and it was like he was inviting me to look at his face as it really was without the mask.

He'd told me all this stuff and got my confidence going, so I decided to tell him about the stuff I had in the bag.

'I'm actually looking for a circus. For my granddad, who might have worked in the circus. Not this one, but anyone. I reckon circus people know each other.'

He couldn't have had a clue what I was talking about but he listened.

'Where did you last see this granddad of yours?'

'I've never seen him.'

'What was he called? Why are you checking for a circus?'

'He was called Josh Rabbit, I think.'

'Josh? We'll find Josh for you.'

He rang up the police and asked them if there were any circuses in town and they said there was a booking for one on a common in a week's time but there was none there now.

I showed Das the plastic plaque and the wooden clown with the umbrella pocket and the note.

'It's good to have something to look for. We'll go to the circus if you want to stay the week and we'll find Josh. We'll track down his strong-man arse.'

four

When Das dug into his coat pockets or trouser pockets, his hand would come out with a wodge of notes, twenty pounders, fifties, tens, fives, in scrunched up bundles and he'd throw them on the table and then sort them out. He didn't mind that I was looking.

The taxi business must be good, I thought, even though, like in the documentary there was war in the cabbie world and someone was bound to die! Das used to count the cash after heaping it up on a little table he had in the centre of his front room. It was always hundreds, sometimes even a thousand pounds.

I saw that the first day and then the next and the next.

'Why don't you go out?' Das asked me.

I said I had nowhere to go, but he brought me a key to the front door that day and he gave me fifty quid.

'Go see a film and grab a fast food, youth, but eat it slow or it'll hit you like a belly-flop,' he said.

I went into the town and I did see a film and I did get some food and I came back to the house. I had got the direction in my head, the turnings to the right and left and worked out the way to the town centre like a map.

I was in Das's house for ten days before things began to happen. He never troubled me. I had everything. A good room with a bed. He got me jeans and shirts my size and I used to wear one of his leather jackets, which was big but warm. I never asked no questions and he came and went from the house all day and all night. One night he rang the bell. I was asleep and came down the stairs. I didn't like to open the door, but he was knocking now

'Rashid! It's me.' It was Das, but his voice was hoarse. I turned on the hall light and opened the door. It was Das, but he had blood dripping through his rasta locks and down his face, and his coat was gone and his shirt was torn. Instead of shades he had big black bulges and cuts around his eyes.

I didn't say anything and he staggered to the bathroom and washed his head, and the blood ran red into the bath from the gash in it.

'They bust up the car and took my keys and money and everything.'

He was unsteady on his feet and he stumbled, clutching a towel.

'Shall I call a doctor?' I asked.

'No, no, no!' he was emphatic. Then he said, 'The car is insured, but that don't save my life. I told you my prediction.'

Then he dropped at the bottom of the stairs. He hadn't fainted, but was too weak to walk. I helped him to his bed. He bled all over the pillow and sheets and didn't care.

I didn't sleep good that night because I thought whoever done it would come back for Das, but they never did. Also I wanted to look after him. He stirred when I called him late in the morning. He was asleep but I wanted to make sure he wasn't like in a coma, which I had heard of. He wasn't in a coma, but he didn't get up that morning or that day, and in the evening he woke up and shouted for me to get him some tea.

'You are the angel come to save me,' he said.

I got him the tea and he struggled out of bed, but felt dizzy and went back to it.

'They beat me up and wasted my car,' he said.

'Who?'

'The taxi wars. They thought I showed them up with that car chase thing, you know when I bumped the guy. They've been waiting for weeks and now they laid a hit on me. But they got hit too. We got some baad maan too.'

'Because you showed them up on telly?'

'That's just an excuse. It's always about money or women.'

In the next few days I did the shopping and the

cooking. Dr Bronco kept getting calls till the tape on the answer machine was full.

Das calls me upstairs and says, 'Rash, boy, me don' like feh ask you dis, but you got to do some work for me, maan.'

'You tell me what,' I said, meaning that I'd like to do anything for him.

'I'm going to tell you something. I want you to carry little packets I give you to the addresses that I give you. Go by bus, don't take any cabs.'

Behind the kitchen there was a bike and I took it down the bike shop and had it cleaned up. Das gave me the cash for that and to buy some maps and get familiar with the town. It was like a treasure hunt.

'I'm sending you out to trusted places. You just got to drop off the stuff.'

Das had a back room behind his bedroom upstairs where he kept his CDs and his books and he didn't care for me to go in there and I respected his house, so I didn't bother. But now he invited me into it. And the secret was not the CDs.

In the corner of the room he was weighing out what looked like dried up grass from a large pillow-case into little plastic packets.

'This is the weed of the ganja seed. The best,' he said.

I knew it was drugs.

'I don't write addresses on envelopes. You've got to

remember where you are taking them, so you can only take as much as you can memorise. Then come back for the next lot, right?'

The first day I went out by bus and the next. Then I took the bike out. I had only ridden a bike in the park, when my mum hired one. This Slough, the town is all over the place, with long distances and little flat estates on hills, and motorways and a lot of confusion. Not like a real city at all. But I learnt my way round and was well pleased that I could do something for Das.

'You're savin' my life, my brother,' he said. 'They put me out of the taxi business till my car is fix and that could take months with body work. And in the weed business, if you don't deliver when they want, they stop calling. Other maan take advantage and move into your territory and steal your regulars. Is all turf.'

The job itself was strange. The customers were usually surprised to see me. I'd just knock or ring and ask for a person by name. When they came to the door, I'd say, 'Dr Bronco's medicines,' and give them the packet.

Das had his own philosophy. He didn't think what he was doing was wrong.

'You must see I don't smoke cigarettes. It's poison and it could kill you, but I take Bronco weed which is good for asthma. It's illegal, you know why?'

'Because it's drugs?'

'You see how they teach you them things? What drugs? This is a natural thing. It's Jah's gift to mankind, to spread peace and take away aggression. But you know why them call it drugs?'

I shook my head.

'The people who make tobacco cigarette. They earn billions of dollars from it. If ganja were freed up, then people would stop smoking killer tobacco and the tobacco people would be ruined. So they pay the governments to keep cigarettes and tobacco going, even if it kill people with cancer and lung things.'

He believed what he was saying.

'But you mustn't smoke anything. You too juvenile,' he said. 'And you don't need to chill, you already chilled. See you? You got so much troubles and you don't business with it.'

By this time I had told him all about myself. The truth. As much as I knew about where Mum had got to and about my granddad dying and I even told him that I had attacked Frankie and run. And I told him about Abu the beard and the takeover bid on my mum's flat. He was well edified by that.

When Das sent me round the next day with packets to deliver to several addresses, he looked worried. 'You're not becoming a dealer. I'm not getting you into that, because a dealer is me, you have to make profit by it and you aren't making no profit, just doing a normal job,' he said.

He was talking to himself maybe. Trying to convince himself that he wasn't getting me into evil.

There was money in it. Bronco would weigh the stuff, which looked like dried leaves round stalks, into little plastic bags and I'd take them round. I got to know the city pretty well and I handled money, good-looking money. I always brought it back to Das who said he was now being pressured by the big boys who gave him the stuff in the first place and he'd spent some of their money and if he didn't return it he would get smashed up even worse. So that's why he hadn't stopped the trade and had to send me out. I said I was obliged.

It was Das who after twelve days remembered the circus. He said he couldn't move but he'd call one of his mates at the cab company and they'd drive me round. It was nice of him. I took the dumbbell with the names scratched on it and went with the friend he had called for six that evening.

The days were still short and it got dark before six. It was a long ride and the driver, who was Das's friend seemed to know some things about me – nothing important, just that I was Das's mate.

We got to the circus and my jaw dropped. Das hadn't done his enquiries right, man. In the field was the circus tent and the big caravans and the lights and everything, but the big board above the tent and the sides of all the large caravans said:

CHINESE STATE CIRCUS.

'We better turn round and go home,' I said.

'I thought you were going to see the circus,' the driver friend said.

'I just came to check the name,' I said.

'To what? Living with Das is driving you crazy. You smoke his weed or what?'

He was only annoyed for a moment. Then I told him that I was looking for a relative who used to work in the circus, but this was the wrong circus. The Chinese wouldn't know anything about him and Das should have asked the police for a British circus.

He had wasted his time, but the driver-friend was ready for it and he drove me back to Das's place and Das gave the friend a bottle of whisky which he drank most of just sitting there through the evening.

'And if your mother's name is Rabinovitch, then her father's name was also Rabinovitch, but you can see why he changed it to Rabbit.'

'I can't,' I said.

Das and his friend glanced at each other. It was as if they knew why.

'Because he didn't want the hassle of being called Rabinovitch. That's a Jewish name. Like, clearly. So the poor bastard, lifting horses in the circus has to call himself Rabbit to pretend he's British. What a fate. Run, Rabbit, run.'

'What a country,' said the friend who was also Asian.

'You mean he was kind of in disguise?' I asked. 'As Josh Rabbit?'

It was a few days after this that Das sent me to Davinia. He said she was the 'beezneez'. I didn't get it then, that he actually meant that she was doing his business. He sent me out with a canvas bag full of stuff. I slung it on my shoulder and was off.

She was wearing shorts, and the first thing I noticed about her, was her knees. They were shiny and red in bits like apples. I took her the bag and she took it into the kitchen and asked me to come with her. Then she takes a wodge of dosh out from under one of them sitting statues with folded legs, them Buddha ones. But this one had got a bit black from being brass. There were lots of notes, but they were all crumpled up, as though money didn't matter. She stuffed the lot into my hand. I said, 'OK,' and I was going when she said she'd like me to wait a minute while she dealt with the stuff, to give Das a report like. I said I was busy but she knew I was just putting it on to be important, like. She said, she didn't appreciate taking deliveries from strangers and that she had to get to know me because I could be anyone, a policeman or anything. So I stayed. Sat down.

She took the stuff that I'd just given her and spread

it out on a table covered in little plants, and then she gave me a beer from her fridge whose door was kept shut with an elastic band. I said I didn't normally drink beer.

'This is not normally,' she said. 'You've only just met me.'

She was thin, spiky, with a sharp nose and above the shorts wore a loose shirt beneath which I could see she didn't wear any bra. Her thighs were thin and slightly hairy and when she sat on the stool as I was drinking the beer I could see her knickers and turned away, because it was embarrassing.

Mum always dressed good and she didn't have dosh, but she shaved and bathed and scented herself. Davinia had not looked after her looks, guy, but she was ugly gorgeous. I don't know if you know the type. She had long teeth which would normally be ugly, but they attracted attention and reminded me of a horse and I liked that. And then she had brown hair which looked like she'd cut it herself.

She asked me about myself. I told her just a bit.

'So no one knows you're here?'

'Das does.'

'Not in this town. In the world. Does anyone know where you are?'

'Yeah, sure, lots of people know I'm in the world. My mum. I don't know where she is, but she must know.'

'If she doesn't care, then it's not worth her know-ing.'

'I thought about that too,' I said. 'I think about it all the time. But look, if I started believing that, then the best thing for me to think is that she's dead. Then it's not that bad in one way, which is that she hasn't forgotten me and left me alone. But it's bad in the way that I'll never see her again, unless there is a heaven and I get to it.'

Davinia laughed. 'There's no heaven. It's right here if there is,' she said. 'We call it karma. You're an Indian, you should know.'

'I'm a Muslim,' I said.

'You're more than that. You are unique. I'd love to be like you. I'd love to be you.'

'I don't think you would,' I said. I didn't know what else to say.

'Now tell me your full name again.'

I told her.

'That's the only sad thing. It's a great name, Rashid Rashid. That's the only thing I would regret.'

I didn't understand what she was talking about and she was a bit crazy, but soothing crazy, hypnotising crazy. She had a singing up and down in her voice which made you want to listen to her.

'I'd better go. Das might have more work for me.'

She smiled.

'I don't pay him nothing to live there. It's free,' I

said, explaining why I wanted to work for Das.

'You don't owe. That's what's beautiful. You are perfectly balanced Rashid Rashid. On the one hand Rashid, on the other hand Rashid. Young enough for innocence, old enough to look after yourself. Here, feel this.'

She leaned over close to my face and took my finger and pressed it down on the centre of her forehead.

'What?'

'It goes in.'

'Damn right. There's a hole there.'

'A hole? In your forehead.'

'Yes.'

'You were in a crash?'

She laughed. 'No man. I made it myself.'

She took me by the hand and led me to her bedroom. It had a mattress on the floor and silver stars and planets, like transfers all over the ceiling. She went to a bookshelf and pulled out a big old book.

She pointed to the bed to sit down. Then she showed me the book, turning the pages for me to look at the pictures. It was about Egypt, ancient Egypt and the book was about making holes in your skull. There were pictures of skeletons with holes drilled in their foreheads.

'That's what I'd like to be. An ancient Egyptian. That's why I did it.'

'You did it yourself?'

'Right. Bull's-eye. Or rather, third eye. I took a drill and drilled the hole in my forehead.'

'Didn't it hurt?'

'The skin, the surface bleeds a bit, but you put some herbs on it and it doesn't get infected. You've got to get through the bone.'

'Water would get in when you have a bath, and germs and everything,' I said.

'That's right, man. The world would enter your head. That's the risk you have to take.'

I thought about what Davinia had said and I asked Das about her.

'She's a nice lickle gel,' he said. 'Slightly crazy, you know that way? But she's bust since she leave her man. I should send her some money by you.'

I was happy to go back and see her. I was curious about her and maybe something more. I took her the money which she pocketed without a word.

I saw her almost every day after that. She used to be on the computer most of the time.

'Das tells me you're looking for your grandpappy,' she said.

'Yes, I am.'

'What was his name?'

'I don't really know, but he called himself Rabbit.'

'That's too vague. What did he do? Did he do anything special – like spot UFOs or anything?'

'He used to lift horses.'

'That's good,' she said and went to the computer.

She typed in 'Horse-lifters'.

Nothing came up. The message on the screen said that there was no such thing. Then she tried horse hoisting and other such words but what we got back was rubbish.

'Your grandpappy's profession doesn't exist.'

'It does. He was a strong man in a circus but I don't know which circus.'

'That gives us a clue,' she said, and she typed in something to do with strong men. The Internet was happier with that and sent back hundreds of files with pictures of strong men and news about competitions.

'This stuff is for perverts,' she said. 'Let's try "circus",' she said and started banging away at her computer.

She found a lot of stuff.

'There's a lot of people about who are into circuses. You don't have any names?'

'I got his name.'

'Yeah, Rabbit. It doesn't work.'

'I've got more names,' I said. I was thinking about the dumbbell and the scratchings on it.

'What are they?'

She might have been getting close. I said I'd go and get them.

I used the key to get into the house because Das didn't answer the bell. That was funny. He was too cut up and not yet strong enough to wander out, but he was gone. The house was silent and dark and empty.

I thought he must have stepped out and I got my bag of clues – the clown statue and the dumbbell. Maybe Davinia could sort something out from those.

As I got to the street I noticed Das's car was gone too. So, sure, he must have driven off.

I went back to Davinia's and she was still playing with the computer.

I gave her the dumbbell with the scratched plating, the names.

'Big Ben. Must have been a circus giant. We can get hold of him, for sure.'

She fed the name into the computer and it came up, in ten minutes, with a hundred articles on repairing the clock in London, famous all over the world.

Nothing about any big boy of the circus.

'I tell you what I did find,' she says. 'I got a guy who wants help on the web to start a museum of British Circus. He doesn't give an address or phone number, but gives a bank number and I called them up and it's a bank in Leicester, so that's where he must be operating from. A museum – he must know stuff from the past. He calls himself Big Top.'

'Big Top? He might know Big Ben,' I said.

'It's no joke, Rashid. Big Top is your hope.'

We were thinking what to do about this hope when fate kind of walked in, or rang the bell or something. In actual fact, the phone rang and Davinia got it and listened. She put it down almost immediately.

'That's it. You can't go home. Back to Das.'

'Why not?'

'He's been busted. Police have taken him away. I'm going to pack some things and go too.'

'Go where?'

'I don't know. Isn't that beautiful?'

'No,' I said. I was a bit panicked. She knew it.

'And you have to come with me. There's nowhere for you to go but outward.'

'All my stuff is there, my clothes,' I said.

'Don't be materialistic. Forget it. Your freedom is more valuable.'

She started putting clothes and books in a big cloth bag.

Then she chucked the bag on the bed.

'I've got to get that stuff,' I said.

'No chance, they'll nab you.'

I didn't know what to do.

'Listen, Rashid Rashid. Das is going to be inside for a long time. His friends will see to that. They sent the police round. Now I've got to run. Same as you, like you told me. The friends know I exist, they'll maybe pick me because I've helped Das out in the past. If you go back there, they'll take you in. You'll get sent into care. So you better come with me.'

I nodded. I hadn't told her about the grievous assault on Frankie. Suppose he was dead, and they were calling it murder?

She left her bag and everything. She went to her computer and kissed it. She spoke to it. Then she left her front door open and she took my hand to cross the street.

'We're walking into the future.'

'What about money? I've only got the cash I picked up for Das this morning. It's his.'

'Yours now. And I've got a bit. But we shouldn't have any money at all,' she said. 'It's against the rules. But you don't know the rules, I haven't told you the rules, so it's OK.'

We went straight to the railway station and Davinia, or Daffy, which is what Das called her, didn't want to buy tickets. She took me straight onto a train.

'We'll busk it,' she said. 'Can't waste what little you've got.'

'I can't go back to London,' I said.

'We're only passing through. There are ten million people in London,' she said. 'But I know what you mean, it's a crowd in which you can't get lost.'

In London we bought a burger and coffee each, even though she said she never ate that stuff. We walked in a park and she wolfed it down.

'Wait for me, I'll be back as soon as I can,' she says.

'Where are you going?'

'Don't worry about it, just sit in the park and watch the squirrels. But you've got to have faith. Wander about if you like, but meet me here in an hour or two. I'll be back.'

She kissed me and left. I watched her go out of the gates of the park and down the Bayswater Road.

Daffy didn't come back for hours. Maybe it was some kind of trick. Or maybe she was mad. The stuff she was saying made some sense, but it was mad.

I waited and she did come back even though she took two or three hours. She was wearing jeans and a shirt and shades and new shoes.

'Daffy, I didn't recognise you.'

'It's because I'm not Daffy, I'm someone new, young man. Come on, we're going on the train. Out of London. Your new life awaits you. Every moment is new. With the next big money I can hustle, we buy a computer and go through the looking glass.'

It was my turn. We went into a clothes shop and she bought me two sets of clothes – like everything from a T-shirt to trousers and shoes. She paid with cash.

'I thought you didn't have any money,' I said.

'I didn't. I got some. I had nothing but my pride to sell.'

'How did you sell it?'

'It doesn't matter. I'm starting a new memory with new secrets.'

I didn't say nothing, but she had quite a lot of money.

'So where then?'

'To find Big Top. In Leicester.'

We went to another train station and took the train to Leicester.

'How do we find Big Top?'

'We've got to establish ourselves first,' she says.

Davinia bought a *Leicester Mercury* and went to the phone booth. Then we got in a taxi and she gave the guy an address.

It was a quiet road with trees and real houses. When we got out and paid the cab there were lots of Indians on the streets, kids and older people. There was a Muslim guy waiting for us by the gate of a house. I knew that by his furry cap.

'Miss . . . er . . . Daffy?' he asked as we got out. 'I told you it's not ready yet. My brother was supposed to finish painting it, but he had to go off to Pakistan. Just warning you.'

'You already warned me,' she said.

We followed the geezer into the house and into the flat on the ground floor which was divided into two. We were at the back of the house and the door was at the side and came out under a staircase. There was only a tiny sitting room, with half of it under the staircase and then a bedroom, a kitchen and a yard with an outside toilet. He was right about the painting. The walls had been scraped and there was no furniture. And on the floor was just one thing – an old lonely computer.

'It just needs two coats. I'll give it you for ten pounds less a week,' the guy said.

'Make it free for two weeks and I'll paint it for you. I'm a very professional decorator. You won't get a better bargain.'

The landlord thought about it. He was a young guy with a big scar across his cheek and when he took his cap off to scratch his skull I could see he had thinning hair on his head even though he wasn't old.

'Do a good job and I'll give you three weeks free. How about that? I am not a businessman, I want to see you and your son happy. If your luggage is coming from the station, I got a van. And you can even use the old computer in there.'

'His dad's bringing our stuff by truck,' she lied.

When he was gone, she says, 'Let's get a mattress and some sheets.'

I can tell you, you can set up a gaff in a day. We got a second-hand mattress, and pushed it down the Narborough Road on a rickety old trolley which the second-hand furniture man gave us.

I never thought I was destined for this kind of shamefulness. Like a tramp or a gypsy, I was pushing a pink mattress down a pavement with a woman who wasn't anything to me.

Then we went to the BHS and she bought up more stuff than we could carry. Pots and pans and kettles and sheets and pillows and that. We spent money like water. But she said she had plenty. She tucked it in her knickers.

'It's going fast. I thought it would be my last outing.'

'Outing where?'

'For the money, Rashid. Grow up. I had to do things for it. You let them chat you up in Bayswater or some place. Then you tell them you're not on the game, but you'll go with them and do whatever they want because you're hungry. They love amateurs. And most of them can tell if you are or not. Three Arabs. No more questions. I feel sick about it.'

It didn't hit me till then that there was only one bed in our new flat. The man at the second-hand shop said he'd send the settee and the two chairs when his van came back, if it came back that afternoon.

It couldn't have come back. We went and bought a TV.

To tell the truth, a panic gripped the centre of my stomach. Let her not be mad, I was thinking, not mad. But she didn't seem mad. She was serious.

'Put on your new clothes and get those off,' she said.

Actually I was dying to try on the shoes and that, so I took the bags and was going to the yard when she says, 'What's the matter, change here.'

I didn't know what to say and I didn't want to get shown up as a shy guy, so I just took my kit off and got into the new stuff, turning my back to her. She wasn't looking at me as I took my knickers off 'cause I turned round to make sure. She was playing with her toes.

'That's smart,' she said and kissed me, and then she took my old clothes into the yard and put them in a pile outside the loo and set fire to them.

'It's symbolic,' Daffy said. 'Symbols become as important as real things as you grow up.'

'It's smokolic,' I said. The shirt and jeans were burning with a lot of black smoke coming off them. But now it was dark and the smoke went up into the dark sky over our yard.

'That's yesterday in flames, the smoke flying at your throat.'

She may have been crazy but she was fascinating. I had never met anyone like her, except my mum. But my mum was cleaner. Daffy could guess what I was thinking most of time.

'I'm not old enough to be your mum,' she said.

'How did you know I was thinking of how old you are?'

'Because I can read you. I would have been twelve

with a baby if I was your mum. But when we go for the school interview I'll dress up older and say I'm your mum.'

The sofa and chairs didn't arrive. Daffy said to sleep with her in the bed and I did. But I couldn't sleep. What she'd done is turned the light out and taken all her clothes off and got into the bed with me. There was no curtain and so the light of the sky and the night was coming through the window and I could see her against the window as she got into bed. She was thin and beautiful and I couldn't help my heart thumping up against my ribs.

At first, she pretended to turn over and sleep. Then she thrust her bum towards me and I could feel her skin against my knee.

'You've never slept with a girl have you?' she says.

'No,' I said.

'But you like it?' All this with her back still turned to me and the sweet sweaty smell of her body under the duvet we'd bought.

'Yes.'

'Do you know what you want to do with me?' she asks.

'I think so,' I said but I was choking on the words because my heart was thumping in my throat now.

She turned to me and put one arm under her head and stroked my hair with the other.

'That would be starting a new chapter, wouldn't it?'

'Yes.'

I could see her breasts now. They were too small to flop, but they weren't standing up, like pyramids, like in the photos you see.

'You want to look at me, don't you, Rashid Rashid?'

'Yeah.'

She pulled the duvet off her and sat up and stroked her own hair and her breasts fell outwards from her ribs which were clear under her skin.

'Not much to see, but you still like it?' she said. 'I wish it was my first time. Go on. You can kiss me if you like, just gently, but I think that's the lot.'

I did kiss her and she pulled my head back with her hand on my forehead. She goes, 'Enough, now sleep.'

'I can't,' I said.

'You want to get me in trouble.'

'Not really,' I said. 'I came with you myself, didn't I?'

'Look, Rashid. I'm sorry. This is unfair to you, isn't it?'

I wasn't shy or scared any longer. But I knew I had to stop.

'Do you know where I got the money? Real money? I've still got almost all of it?'

'No,' I said. 'And I don't want to know.'

'You want to be my lover, you should know.' She moved out from under me and propped her head up on her arm on the pillow. 'Three young Arab guys.

101

One after the other. Each one offered me more money than the last to be his girlfriend. They said they'd buy me a flat and clothes.'

'So, why didn't you go with them?'

'To go somewhere new and start again? That would have been part of the game. But I'd left you in the park and I'd told you I'd come back.'

Then she leans over and kisses me gently on the lips. We'd been snogging, tongues and teeth and everything, but now she'd turned gentle.

'We've had a big day. Let's sleep. You should curl up to me, but sleep, yeah?'

I said yeah. Maybe I was even relieved that she'd stopped there. I put my arm around her gently breathing body and I must have fallen asleep or passed into sleep and then come out of it and each time, just half awake, I was amazed that there was a naked woman lying there next to me.

I didn't really know her. I had come here looking for some geezer called Big Top. It was all bewildering, except I wasn't bewilderable. When I woke up and she was still curled up under the duvet, I looked at her, I didn't see the face I remembered her having. She was new. She had a big black beauty spot on her cheek and I hadn't seen it, it had just been there and I hadn't taken it in. Just there, bang on the cheekbone and big too. Black and green, a twist of a green centre in the spot, dark green like the colour of wine bottles if you looked very close, which I was doing while she slept.

'We must find a new life for ourselves,' she said over breakfast. We'd done the shopping and it was all lying on the kitchen floor because there was no fridge, but she wasn't mean with it. It was bacon and eggs and tomato and fried bread.

'You eat bacon? You don't have to, but I am,' she said.

'My granddad didn't allow it in the house, but Mum did, even though she was Jewish. She thought it made you strong.'

'Alice fell down a rabbit hole,' she said.

Someone else might have thought she was crazy, but I'd seen the video. They showed it to us at school – *Alice in Wonderland* – so I knew what she was on about.

'And the next time she went through the looking-glass, because there were other worlds out there and she wanted to be in them.'

'But she didn't come from Slough to Leicester. This isn't Wonderland, is it. How do we get to find Big Top?' I asked.

'I'll go to the bank that his website said to send the money to and ask there. Leave it to me. But we can get on with other things.'

'Like what?'

'Like you never slept with a girl before and last

night you did. And you learned something. I don't know what. That's up to you. Take it easy. More things are bound to happen. We are going to walk through the looking-glass, or go down the rabbit hole.'

'I reckon that's a silly way of looking at it,' I said. 'That Alice stuff is old-fashioned. You want to be something for now. Alice is books, not even TV.'

'You're too smart for your own good. And you're wrong. Now that everyone in the world can talk to each other on the Net, we've killed distance and killed time. Nothing is old-fashioned. Everything is here, now. So let's see how smart you turn out to be at a tough Leicester school.'

'And what will you do? Will you sign on?'

'I'll look for ways of getting rich.'

'Why can't I look for ways of getting rich too?'

The next day she got a computer and started banging away at it.

'What are you doing?' I asked

'I am Alice,' she said.

'What do you mean? Are you pretending to be Alice on the computer?'

'No, you fool I *am* Alice, from moment to moment. She who was dead when they closed the books and is now come.'

'Yeah? Does anyone know you're Alice?'

'The citizens of Wonderland do.'

'And where are they?'

'In the box, look.'

She got up from the table and let me sit at the computer. I looked at the screen. There was a letter written to her on it, addressed to Alice.

Dear Alice,

The knave of hearts he stole the tarts and the bum, he ate them all.

Your friend,

The Queen of Hearts

'Is this person mad?' I asked blankly.

'No, far from it.'

She stepped over to the computer and began to reply to the e-mail.

Dear Queenie of Hearts,

Spot of bother. Alice has gone back to the world of the living. Sorry, will be in touch.

Alice

'Least I can do,' she said almost to herself.

I knew enough about reading screens to see that she had designed her own website and called it WonderAlice dot com. It had flowers and hearts and spades on it. Yuk. I told her I could do a better job and she just hit me on the shoulder and said, 'Crap. There's more letters.' She read them. I did too over her shoulder. They didn't make any sense to me.

Dear Alice,
   I gave the Sheriff a good knockabout at High Noon. Stay merry.
Your outlaw friend

'Good,' she says, and checks the next one.

Dear Alice,
There was a man from St Ives
Who had seven nagging wives
In order to keep them happy
He had to live seven lives
Best wishes,
Don Quixote

'Got it. Here's a good one,' she says.

Dear Alice,
Ding dong
Ding dong
Ding dong
Ding dong
Ding dong

Eleven is right and seven is wrong.
Quasimodo

There were more, but I got fed up of looking at them.

'You carry on a game with nutters,' I said.

'Now you know who I really am,' she said. She was smiling but I swear she was serious.

She started replying to the letters and in twenty minutes she was done.

'What about the Circus Museum?' I asked

'I sent the guy a letter,' she said. 'Read it.'

She brought it up on screen.

Dear Big Top,

I have a wooden statue and a very rare dumbbell signed by twenty circus artistes of the past. These are priceless antiques for your Circus Museum. If you are interested, I am in Leicester.

Yours,

Alicia Rashid

'That'll lure him out. If he wants to see your things, he can't see them over the Internet. He'll have to meet us face to face and then we can track down Josh Rabbit or Big Ben or one of the others and you can have your grandpappy back.'

There were more e-mail letters the next day. Alice

was lying in bed and she asked me to read them out, so I did.

Dear Alice,
You gave me hyacinths a year ago
Yet when we came back from the rose garden
Your arms full and your hair wet,
I could not speak.
And then again
With a dead sound on the final stroke of nine.
How are things?
Humpty Dumpty

'Got that,' she said. 'Next.'

'There can't be anyone really called Humpty Dumpty. These people are having you on,' I said.

'They're not. They are real people with real needs. Don't bother your head about it. Go and steal a *Yellow Pages* and get a map of Leicester while you're about it.'

I was getting curious about this game but I wasn't going to ask, because that's what she wanted. I did as I was told. I went to an Asian shop and asked the old guy if he had a map of Leicester. I bought it. There was a public phone box in the shop, behind a wooden partition. I had spotted that there was a *Yellow Pages* in there, with a string tying it to a nail. I wrenched the nail out, put the *Yellow Pages* book in the carrier bag with the map and was about to leave the shop when the old guy says, 'Don't take that one. I'll give you a new one.'

I felt like running, because he'd caught me stealing his book, but something in his voice told me he wasn't going to do anything to me. He brought out a brand new *Yellow Pages* from behind the counter and handed it to me. I gave him back his dirty thumbed one.

I said, 'Thanks,' feeling a bit stupid, but he said he had fifty of them, and he didn't bat an eyelid.

I left in a hurry.

Alice, which is what she wanted to be called, started looking through the *Yellow Pages*. I checked to see what she was doing. She'd turned to the public houses and was making a list of them and their addresses.

'I'll give you a clue,' she said. 'In all of those letters there's a number, which is a time of day.'

'Like High Noon? Twelve o'clock?'

'Brilliant. Right first time. But of course they are not written as times on the clock. They are just a number.'

'And what's the rest of it? As if I can't guess?'

'Go on then.'

'It's the names of pubs, isn't it?'

'You should be on the quiz shows on telly, you'd make a bomb. You got it. But do you know the names of the pubs? Which pubs would they be? These punters come up with new puzzles each time. Humpty

Dumpty is very clever. She writes great clues.'

'It's a girl?'

'A woman, please.'

'Sure, but why is she so smart?'

'Because I've got to figure out the name fresh each time. That letter – *When you came back from the rose garden, your arms full and your hair wet . . .* – that's a line from a T. S. Eliot poem.'

'So the pub is called the Rose Garden or something?'

'Could be, but there isn't a pub called the Rose Garden in Slough. Nah, she meant The Floral Arms – arms full of flowers, get it?'

I got it. I went back to the other letters on the screen to see if I could guess them. I got the Ding dong. Five times.

'That's The Five Bells? To meet at eleven o'clock.'

'If it's that simple, the cops will break the code,' she said.

'I wouldn't have got it in a million years if you hadn't told me. What was the Don Quixote one?'

'Oh, that's simple, that's The Windmill because there's a famous windmill in the Don Quixote story. And the other one? The Sheriff of Nottingham is obviously The Robin Hood, and it wouldn't take the cops a million years to work that one out either. Though given the ninnies they pick, it might take longer.'

'Or never,' I said.

'There's no such thing as never,' said Alice.

'What do you mean? Of course there is. When something doesn't happen, ever.'

'That's what's impossible. Everything that's possible has got to happen. If you flip a coin for ever and ever and it comes down either heads or tails, then very soon it will come down heads twice in a row, won't it?'

'Yes, that's obvious.'

'And then three times in a row, or four or five? Before it comes down tails again?'

'That's possible.'

'Then if you go on for ever there might come a time when it comes down heads a hundred times in a row. Not today or tomorrow or next year, but just once in a million years?'

'It's possible.'

'If it comes down heads a hundred times, then it can come down heads, a million times,' she said. 'And if the coin thrower is God and he keeps at it for ever, then it will be possible and will happen more than once.'

'What's the point you're making?'

'Everything's possible. Natural, supernatural . . . '

'So you believe in ghosts?' I asked.

'I bet you say you don't believe in them but you're still scared of them.'

'You know what I'd do if I saw a ghost? I'd ask it to hang about while I fetched a video camera and then I'd ask the ghost to pose for me. Once I had got that on tape I'd be the only one in the world to have conclusive proof, like the freaks who think they've seen men from outer space and that. Then I could sell it and it would be like winning the lottery – like a movie in which a witch actually appears. That would be so cool and I could be frightened all the way to the bank.'

Alice frowned. She didn't like it

'Don't say that, Rashid Rashid. Please. You don't mean it. You'd make money out of a miracle?'

'Sure. That's what they're good for.'

'You can't make money out of ghosts and the supernatural. It's just wrong. We've destroyed everything else we touch, we have to leave that untouched by money and bargaining and sales.'

'That's just your opinion,' I said. 'Anyone who can get hold of money – in an honest way, I mean, without hurting no one, they'd go for it, wouldn't they?'

'No. Wrong. Sometimes you turn your back. I'm going to show you something,' she said. 'I could be rich.'

'How?'

'I'll show you.'

She made some quick passes at the keyboard, and there on the screen was another website.

'Right. I just have to pick an address from this book and ask for money. Let's take ten of them. Watch.'

She clicked a button and a lot of names and addresses came up.

'Right let's have Abbie, Adolf, Alfie, Arch, Aristo, Atilla. Is that enough? I'm going to write them the same letter, only they don't know it.'

She wrote it:

My dearest ____

She pressed the mouse button and all the different names got filled in.

I can't really talk now, but I've been in trouble, that's why I haven't been in touch. I can't explain what I've been through yet, but will soon because I want to share it with you more than with anyone else. I know you'll understand. I don't really want it now, but if I needed it sweetheart, would you be able to help me out with a small sum of money? Up to say a hundred? Just say yes or no, with no strings. I wouldn't ask if I wasn't desperate, but I may not need it at all.
With all my love,
Dee

She sent them off.

The next day she got the idea that I should be at school instead of hanging about the flat.

I wasn't sure but she said it would be a gas.

We went down to look over the fence of the local school and check out the kids coming through the gate. There were a lot of Asian kids and they looked raggy, not like the lot at my school who just wore *Addies* and *Nikes*, like the boys from the hood. These kids looked like the boys from the 'burbs.

'Looks sad,' I said to Alice.

'Sad or not, you got to go to school.'

'We're not staying long,' I said.

'Even if we're only here for a few months, some-one's bound to notice you and report that you're too young to be knocking about and not going to school. Once you're registered there you can play philosophical truant.'

'What does that mean?'

'It means feeling smarter than the teachers and not going to school regularly.'

When we got back to the flat, which was really the space beneath the stairs, she had a message from Big Top the museum man. He was reluctant to come into the open, but he asked for more particulars about the wooden statue and the dumbbell with the signatures.

Alice told me I had to write back and describe it as I liked.

She left me to write it and got back to her own

computer.

The mugs had replied. Five of the six people she'd written to. They all said they'd send her some money. Two of them said they were pretty tight but still they'd like to help her out, and one said if she'd give him her address he'd give her regular cash.

'Why would they send you money?'

'You believe they would, don't you?'

'For what, though?'

'Because people are good. Because they think they know me and they don't. I've done this business before. I've taken money from lonely people and it's not nice.'

I didn't know what she meant, but she explained.

She had come to Slough to be a teacher in a school. Little kids. And a guy came one day to install the computers in the school. They were new, true blue, shiny computers. The guy was called Sebastian.

She said he was funny; not much to look at or a flash dresser but he was kind, at first, and stayed all hours.

Of all the teachers Alice was the brightest. She picked up the computer business – drawing and printing and interacting – before anyone else.

She was straight with me. Part of the reason she was doing it was that she wanted to hit on Sebastian. She would make up computer problems and hang around till he'd done with the kids and they'd work the keyboard together. He had a deep voice, she said, and he'd been a sailor but came out of the Navy and become a computer man.

She made up her mind fast. In a few days Alice had moved in with him and even though she kept her room in the flat she shared with three other girls, she was mostly up his place. That's till they both got thrown out because Sebastian had been going with the landlord's sister, who made a big fuss and smashed the windows when she got jealous. The landlord asked them to go and Alice thought it best so they moved into her room together.

Then Sebastian started staying home and not going to work, asking her to phone up and tell the schools where he should have been working that he was ill.

She didn't like telling them lies, but he didn't care. One day when she began to argue about it, he picked up the phone himself and told the school that he was dead.

Then he started figuring out scams.

Every day he'd think up some new trick. He had set up a thing called Treasure Island on the web and he was good story writer. He wrote that he had been a sailor, which was true and he also wrote that he'd found hidden treasure which, Alice said, may or may not have been true. He had advertised on the web that he had ancient maps of treasure buried in all sorts of places all over the world. If anyone wanted these maps so they could look for the treasure he was selling them cheap because he himself was too old to travel and dig. In fact, he said, he was so old he was about to die and would like to pass on his secrets.

Alice said that a lot of idiots sent him money in the post and he sent them the maps which he made himself, painting on old bits of canvas and rag torn from jackets and coats which he sent Alice out to buy from the Oxfam shop.

That was just one of his swindles. His motto, Alice said, was: 'Fools pay for dreams. The intelligent make them up.'

'He was as cunning as a fox,' Alice said. Zeb, as she called him, was sending his photograph out on the Internet and making friends with girls and spinning them some sob story about how he was in trouble and saying he was broke and had to give up his house and sell his computer because he couldn't raise the last hundred pounds he needed. He would write, 'I'm afraid this is goodbye,' and some of them would feel sorry for him or want him to carry on writing, so they'd send him money through the post or he'd give them the number and they'd put it in his bank. It was easy-peasy.

Some of the women, the poor sad lonely cows, would send him the money with long notes saying how if they didn't trust him they couldn't trust anybody in the world.

To a few of them he even said after a few months of writing every day that he'd meet them in hotels somewhere in the world. They were made for each other and all this. He had no intention of going. He'd ask them to meet him in a hotel and after making them wait there a few days, would send an e-mail saying he was in deep trouble and could they send him the airfare. And a lot of them did. Imagine all those girls waiting in hotels somewhere.

'Hey baby, Zeb is not late, he is a lifetime away,' he would say. 'Maybe next incarnation, yeah? Live in hope and die in despair.'

'So your boyfriend was a slime-ball?' I asked Alice, even though it sounded a good scam.

'I don't know whether I hated him or loved him,' she replied. 'But that trick was not nice. For him with his lovely letter writing manners it was too easy. The man disappears, like the Cheshire Cat. They can't write back ever. He has changed his name on the web and packed up and gone. Only the smile, the triumphant, cheating grin remains.'

But then he got Alice working for him. At first, she didn't think it was right and she fought him. And then he tried to interest her flatmates in the game and started making her jealous, so she gave in.

For the first time, she said, she just tried it as a dare. But then she got hooked.

'In a week, I had twenty guys writing to me and in two weeks there were three hundred. And some of them would send their photographs to download and they were nice looking blokes and I wanted to make Zeb jealous. But that wasn't possible, he was completely cool about it. It was his business. That's how he treated it.'

'Did you start cheating the guys? Like operating the sting and making them wait in hotel rooms for you and getting money off them?'

For a minute she didn't reply. Then she says, 'Yes, I did. He got me into it and I even quit my job. But not just to do this stuff. Something happened at school. This ten-year-old boy brought a knife into school and stabbed another kid who had hit him in the playground the previous day. It was some fight, some matter of honour and the older brother of the knife kid sent him into school to take his revenge and gave him the stupid knife. The brother stood at the school gate with his gang, just in case.

'So this kid goes right ahead and sticks a knife in the other one's ribs. He didn't kill him, but there was a massive row. It was all over the papers and even came on TV, and I was right in it because I was on playground duty and when I saw this gang of teenagers, I rushed to the gate to tell them to clear off. Meanwhile, the stabbing happened.'

'You should have minded your own business,' I said.

'It was my business, Rashid, I was the teacher!'

Any rate, she told me she went to the hospital where the victim was recovering that evening and the sisters of the boy who was stabbed grabbed hold of her and beat the shit out of her. None of it was her fault, but they weren't, like, logic wizards.

Then Alice said she'd had enough of this kind of treatment at school, and though she spent ten days in hospital recovering from the bust ribs that these girls had given her, she spent all the rest of the recovery time at home with Zeb the pleb and got pulled into the business. She can't say how. She was feeling dizzy and weak because her ribs and chest hurt. She said it was like when friends give you your first cigarette and you try it out and the ground doesn't open beneath your feet and the devils don't drag you into hell. You think it's not so bad and you get into it.

Alice said, 'Zeb was very nice to me throughout, looked after me and that. And when the money started rolling in from Lonely of Brooklyn and Abandoned of Paris, then all of us in the flat, my flatmates who we used to call Rag, Tag and Bobtail, we all gave up our jobs and shared the joy of being a gang. Friends against the world.'

She said the feeling that it was wrong just went away. Zeb used to say, 'It's only money we're taking from them,' and, 'Give them their money's worth, girls. Give the no-hopers some hope. Let them think they have captured the most beautiful and loving girl in the world. That's what these guys live for, their dreams.

'In fact,' he said, 'I am willing to bet that even if we tell these geezers, your e-mail lovers, the whole truth, they would still want to be part of it. They are paying for the poetry.'

Alice said they got rich on it . . . and then one day she made the mistake of giving out Zeb's mobile phone number to one of the geezers. He turned up at their house a week or two later and demanded to see her. He was an old bloke and said he'd sent her six hundred pounds and had been conned and wanted it back. He'd traced the phone to the address somehow.

Alice didn't want to answer the door or talk to him, but Zeb got hold of him and thrashed him. Alice tried to stop him beating the geezer up, but Zeb saw him off and put a grievous hurt on him.

'That was it. I felt sick,' Alice said.

It was then that Alice decided to leave. She just stepped out one day, taking a few clothes and a few books with her. She was hoping Sebastian would follow her and look for her so she left clues. She wasn't even going to leave the town. That was when she got talking to Das. She knew him because he drove the cab from the company near their flat and they used to call him when they were coming home from parties at night and that. But this time he saw her crying and asked her what the matter was and he was good to her. She moved into his house for a few days.

It was while she was living in Das's house that she started using his computer, changing herself from Davinia to the secret Alice. She didn't ask for money, she just wrote back to lonely guys. They'd call themselves The White Rabbit and other stuff out of the books.

'After a bit, I thought I'd built up a family and it made me feel good. Clean again, like making up for cheating the lonely men.

And then she told me a funny thing. Before she left Zeb's she wrote to all the guys she'd cheated, all of them, posted a letter saying she had messed them about. Some of them wrote back saying they knew they were being had but didn't mind, as it was something to do.

'Do you get that, Rashid? They wanted to be conned because they had nothing else to do. And some of them sent me their phone numbers and that.'

But now she wasn't earning any money and being Alice was taking up a lot of time, so that's why she got into selling dope. She moved out of Das's place and set up on her own. Which is where I found her.

'So that's how I'm Alice,' she said.

Alice now decided we'd go and pay the school a visit. The head teacher, a woman with short blonde hair and very designer specs, invited us into the office and asked Alice how she was related to me. We had made up the story. She was my sister, we were orphans and we had just returned from Pakistan where I had been in school.

If we had said that I went to school in London they would have checked with my last school and the cops would have come round for me. So we had to make up this story.

The head was intrigued.

'Do tell me a bit of family history, Ms Khan,' she said. 'You must be siblings with only one parent in common.'

'Oh yes,' says Alice. 'We had the same Mum but she died in Pakistan and I came back here and brought Azim with me because he didn't want to stay with his father's people.'

'So have you been in a British school before, Azim?' The head was pretty on the ball with the new name which even I hadn't heard. 'Where?'

We didn't expect such close questioning.

'Yes, in London, but I can't remember the name.'

'Ah, so how old were you when you transferred to Pakistan?'

'Only six,' I said.

'And you've been in school there ever since, Azim?'

'Yes, yes, he has,' said Alice.

'Well, well. Whereabouts in Pakistan were you?'

'Oh, Lahore,' I said, as we'd planned. I knew the name of that city anyway.

'Yes, and what was the name of your school?' Now this one we had thought of. 'St Aloysius,' I said. 'It was Christian and English speaking.'

'I see. And where in Lahore was this school?'

'In the centre. Quite near the centre.'

'So, you've been out of the country for eight years?'

She had done her sums right.

'Yes, miss,' I said.

The head teacher was beginning to look searchingly from Alice to me.

'You've retained a very strong London accent,' she said.

'He spoke English with Mum all the time,' said Alice.

'That's admirable. And tell me, Azim, if that's your real name, what was your class called?'

'Oh it was called 2B. I was in year ten.'

I smiled.

She smiled back.

'That's peculiar, very unusual. Because in Pakistan they call them 'standards'. At your age you would have been in the tenth standard.'

'Yes, that's what I meant. The tenth standard. I was just making it so you could understand it, miss,' I said.

'You needn't,' she said. 'I spent the last year in Pakistan as an advisor on schools to the Pakistani

Government. In Lahore, as it happens – and there's no St Aloysius school there. Now, tell me your name and what you really want and why you're trying to get into my school.'

Alice sprang to her feet and held out her hand.

'We'd better be going,' she said. 'Thank you for seeing us. We take it the answer is *no*.'

'The answer is, I want to know what you are up to. I can have the police round here, you know.'

'I didn't ask you to empty your safe, lady. We just came to get my brother into your worthless school.'

'He's not your brother and you know it. And it doesn't matter about the safe – you know very well that it's against the law to have underage . . . er . . . boyfriends.'

She didn't want to say 'sex'.

We both started to laugh. 'We'll be going then, Mother Teresa,' said Alice and jerked her head to indicate the door.

We ran out of the head's office, through the playground and into the street.

We couldn't stop laughing at the expression on her face when Alice called her school worthless and then when she called her Mother Teresa.

'That's the end of your academic career,' Alice said. 'Unless you go back to London.'

She knew that was impossible. There was nowhere for me to go.

A couple of days later a man came to the door. He was a young fat, Pakistani geezer and he was carrying a stepladder which he'd brought from the back of the van he'd left in the middle of the road with its back doors wide open. Alice answered the door and I was right behind her.

'Yeah?'

'I am the landlord's brother. Sorry, two of us own this place. I want to check the lead on your outside toilet roof, yeah? It's leaking?'

'Of course,' said Alice.

She got her coat and stepped out.

The bloke passed through the front room and saw the computer. He was quite friendly and while he was banging on the roof I watched him.

'What's your name?' he asked.

I told him the truth.

'You a computer freak?'

'Not really.'

'Is your wife, then?'

'I'm too young to be married,' I said.

'I was trying to be polite. Is she your girlfriend?'

'Just a friend and flatmate.'

It struck me just then that he might know the guys at the mosque back in London and now that he knew my real name he'd grass me up.

five

Alice didn't tell me what she would do with the names of the pubs and the times hidden in the computer codes, but it didn't take Einstein to guess. She was taking Das's little packets round to people who'd pick them up at pubs. She was peddling drugs. But now she didn't have any to peddle, so she was getting on the computer and trying to locate the big boys, Das's mates who might be carrying on the business while he was away. I figured that out but didn't say nothing to her.

The next morning she started looking up where the different pubs were and marking them out on the map.

Then she came clean. She said 'You'll have to join the firm. You can solve the big problems. Problem number one is we got nothing to sell. Problem number two is we've got no one locally who wants to buy it. There must be customers in Leicester, but they don't know the game. If we find one or two, the word spreads. The big boys will get in touch with me. I've just got to check twice a day. Meanwhile there's nothing to do but wait for circus man.'

We waited a few weeks in that flat, and then the cash ran out. Alice said she'd heard from one of the big shots. She could get some dope to sell. She set out on her own saying I shouldn't go with her. She came back in a few hours with some cash.

'Did you get some stuff?' I asked.

'And got rid of it fast,' she said. 'We'll get the whole thing going soon. You can spend the next few days researching the pubs.'

She had got the cash to buy the dope but I didn't know where from and it got me thinking.

Whenever we got short Alice would go out and come back with some cash. So what was I to think? Once or twice she went off for the day and once she stayed away overnight, saying she had to leave town to make contacts.

As I watched Alice trying to keep things from me, I began to understand her better. She was like an actor on TV, happier as the character she played than as herself. Perhaps she had even forgotten that she was someone else.

Then one day she brought back a haul of stuff. And she had contacts. Now the messages started coming in and just like she said, the word spread. We started with two or three and then maybe twenty or thirty 'set-ups' as Alice called them, a day.

I'll tell you some of the clues they put in for the

names of pubs. It was like sorting crosswords.

Dear Alice,
This is the man from Banbury Cross.

That was a pub called The White Horse.

Dear Alice
This is the tenth time my girlfriend's run off with
another guy and I could kill him.
Guess who?

That one Alice figured out – it was a jealous fellow
so it was The Green Man.

There were lots of them like that. It was hard work
too. I couldn't go on the drops because I was too
young and couldn't be seen hanging around the bar
and buying drinks. I'd get nicked. So Alice did the
drops and I did the post and the mapping out.

I didn't get fed up with it, but time was running
out. I wasn't getting any further with finding my
granddad or my mum, and I started feeling useless. At
least when I used to go to school and got to play
games with the kids outside Plato House on the estate
in London, I felt I was growing up. But in this place,
with me going only as far as the park and sometimes
into the centre of town to shop, still looking out for
coppers who might have pictures of me sent up from

London or something, I felt like I was the Hunchback of Notre Dame and lived with Alice in prison or at the top of a tower, even though it wasn't a tower but just two rooms in a grubby house.

And then luck struck. Big Top sent Alice a message.

My dear Alice,

Your descriptions of a wooden statuette and a pair of dumbbells don't sound to me as though they are authentic or valuable circus gear. If you have anything else in your possession, I shall be very happy to consider purchasing it at a modest price. As you know I am trying to set up a small museum of circus memorabilia and am very close to receiving funding from the Lottery charities for this work.

Thank you for your offer of free assistance with records and things. I have been inundated with these generous offers and will let you know in due course.

I am etc.

Big Top

Alice wrote back:

Dear Big Top,

As I mentioned we are collectors of circus memorabilia ourselves. We have in our possession:

A lion-tamer's whip from the first Barnum and Bailey circus with the name embossed in gold on the handle.

*A Victorian clown's costume in satin and silk in perfect
condition.*

*The jawbone of one of the first tigers to be brought to a
circus in Britain with a sheet and records showing the
pedigree of the tiger.*

Plates used by jugglers in Victorian travelling circuses.

*. . . and a host of other objects of even more value and
interest.*

*My younger brother, who is merely fourteen is also very
keen to assist with the classification of records in his school
holidays.*

Yours sincerely,

Alice

'But we don't have any of these things!' I said.

'That's the way to make him reply,' she said. 'Wait
and see. He won't be able to resist.'

He wasn't. Big Top replied within the hour.

Dear Alice,

*Your collection sounds absolutely wonderful. Please send
me your address and I shall make arrangements to have
the objects viewed by one of our curators forthwith.*

*Your brother's offer of help with the records I very grate-
fully accept and I shall be in touch as soon as you send me
his particulars: his name, age, school and a photograph if
possible so I can distinguish between all the people who have
volunteered.*

'See, he fell for it straightaway. Now we send him the address and he sends a fellow round. Then we talk to the fellow and find out where Josh Rabbit is. You get to look at all the names and details of strong men in circuses in his registers if he has them. Our best bet, Rashid, my darling.'

She'd never called me her darling before and I think it made me blush.

'We've got to wait for him to get in touch now,' Alice said.

That evening she got a call on the phone but she didn't seem to want to talk about it. I was cooking the meal and she shut the door and sat under the stairs for an hour talking.

She became very quiet and ate the food I'd made in silence.

I felt let down by that, because I thought she said she'd cut herself off from all the 'baggage' of her life as she called it. That she didn't want to know the people who knew her phone number.

I'd been sleeping next to her all this time, but now she said she'd sleep in the front room and I could have the whole bed. I didn't say nothing that night.

After that phone call I said there were some drops to

do, but she pretended she wasn't listening.

'So what's eating you?' I asked.

'Why should something be eating me?'

'That phone call. It's bothered you. Who was it?'

'Rashid, don't ask me silly things.'

'What's silly about that? Who called you? You talked for hours.'

'I talked for five minutes, maybe.'

'It's your Sebastian. Your man. He's tracked you down.'

'Suppose he has. Does that make you jealous or something?'

'Me? Jealous? About what? About you?' I asked.

'Yes, about me.'

'If you think I fancy you. I don't,' I lied.

'And I think you do. And I like you too but you're too bloody young.'

'It's not that. You love him, don't you? Your con man. Bloody crook.'

'This isn't a conversation I want to be in,' Alice said.

Then she didn't say no more but that night she put on a dress she'd bought and said I shouldn't stay up, she'd see me later. She went out. I waited a few minutes and then I followed her.

The centre of town was about half an hour's walk. I followed her but she never suspected it.

I saw her go into a bar and I waited for ten minutes

outside and then I went through the door and looked in.

The bar was crowded out. It was an old and grand place with wooden floors and decorated metal pillars going up to the ceiling. There was a dance floor but no one was dancing. The music drowned out everyone's voices.

Alice was sitting in one of the little booth places with an old man and he was holding both her hands in his. If she had turned round she'd have spotted me.

I had seen what I wanted to see. I pushed off and walked home and got into bed. I heard her come in and sleep on the front couch. I pretended to be asleep.

In the morning Alice was in a funny mood.

'I think we need stuff from the shops,' I said and she knew I was asking for money.

She gave me some notes from her jacket. She didn't say nothing. Then she had another phone call and asked me if I could go out then and get the shopping after she picked up the phone. She was getting rid of me. I said I didn't mind but I did. I went.

'So who was that?' I asked when I got back.

Alice didn't reply.

'Was it Sebastian or was it your old geezer?'

'What old geezer?'

'You know, the one in the bar,' I said. I should have stopped myself. There was no need to give myself away.

'So you followed me?' said Alice.

I said nothing. My turn to not reply.

'Maybe it's time to move on,' Alice said. 'Maybe it doesn't suit you. Maybe I chose the wrong guy to be the Mad Hatter and live with me in Wonderland.'

I think she thought she was threatening me, but I didn't care. We didn't have many rows but here was one coming.

'I didn't ask to play this stupid game. You kidnapped me.'

'Is that what you really feel, Rashid? I thought we were in this together.'

'But in what?' I asked. 'Selling this garbage? Dope peddling?'

'What else is there to do? Do you want to climb mountains? Let's go. Do you want to travel? Let's do it. I tell you something, I used to teach in a school, then I got out of the nine to five – or six to midnight, really. I started writing letters and being a leech and now I enjoy just selling dope, selling dreams. I'm stuck. And I thought I could start like new, but one can't. So I'm facing it. Being Alice the dealer.'

'You can stick with being Alice, but I'm done,' I said. I didn't know I was going to say that, it just came out.

She didn't speak to me for the rest of the day and I wasn't going to give in either, so I went and bought a very noisy video game called Patttaaaaaang! in which you get to be in charge of a whole guerrilla group in the jungle and you've got to fight a war.

The game made a big noise. I turned the computer's volume control full on so Alice would be disturbed and I played for hours. Whizz! Bang! Pow!

Finally, she gave in and looked over my shoulder and pressed one or two buttons and led my army into certain defeat and we both laughed and then she kissed me on the forehead and we laughed at ourselves for having a silly row and ending it this way and I went back to being the Mad Hatter.

We were friends again. She got mad e-mails, all lovey-dovey stuff again which I read when she went out. I knew I shouldn't have asked about the old geezer in the pub. It was her secret and she was ashamed. But at least I knew where she was going when she went out.

One of those evenings I checked her computer and found this. What was strange was that it wasn't written to Alice, the person knew that it was Davinia or Dee or Daffy.

Dear Daffy,

Because I know it's you. I met this person on the net and such is the power of it that she was telling me of a therapist called Alice. Immediately my ears pricked up and my forefinger began to do a mouse-tap. Alice in Wonderland,

moved towns. Why Alice? Why not Eve and then I'd write
to you as Adam. Madam I'm Adam. Did you know that
you can read that backwards and it would be the same?
MadamimadaM. I wanted to ask your advice about a very
nice new fruit I've discovered and a friend has been advis-
ing me to eat. There's no one else in the garden to share it
with. God only pretends to be angry. He isn't really.
Adam

I didn't know what it meant. I put her screen onto
an Ali G. saver, which keeps saying 'Check dis', 'check
dis', 'check dis' in the most irritating voice. Just so
she'd know I'd messed with her computer and her
letters.

When she came back, I could smell the beer and
smoke coming off her. The next evening she dressed
up very carefully. She wore a new top and make-up. I
had never seen Alice with any make-up, but she had
put on eye-shadow and a bit of lipstick. She asked me
how she looked.

'Good,' I said. 'But what are you doing it for?'

'For a change,' she said. 'Alice is a schizo. She has
two sides to her. The slave and the princess. The slut
and the model. Today, she's the princess. You just be
good and don't wait up.'

When she'd gone and I was playing the computer
game there was a ring and a geezer at the door when I
answered.

'Good evening. I am looking for Miss Alice,' he said.

'She's not here,' I said. I didn't want to talk to this bloke. He was an old guy and wore a long checked coat and a cap.

He must be one of the people she was meeting in the pubs in town.

I was going to close the door on him when he said, 'That's unfortunate. I'm only here for the evening and then have to return to Devon. I very much wanted to see her. You don't happen to be her younger brother do you?'

Now the only person she had told that I was her younger brother was the circus man.

'Are you Big Top?' I asked.

'Yes I am. Herbert Astley, the real name.'

He took his cap off.

'I believe you've things to show me. A lion tamer's whip and some outfits and antiques.'

'Come in,' I said. 'But I can't show you those things until Alice comes back. Late tonight.'

'An absolute pity,' he said. 'Can she not be told on the phone that I am here. I came a long way.'

'She hasn't got her mobile,' I said. I didn't want him to slip away. 'But we could find her.'

'That would be great,' said Big Top.

He gave me a card which I put in my pocket and then I led him into town. I didn't know what he'd make of Alice or of the truth that we had told him lies and didn't have any of the stuff he expected to see, but I left that to her. I wanted to ask him if he could find my grandfather for me.

I could see why he called himself Big Top. He had a bald and big head. And as yet he was the closest I had got to knowing who Josh Rabinovitch was and where he was. But as we walked along I felt that I was making progress. I felt that Josh was alive and when I found him and went up to him and said I was his grandson he would welcome me and if he'd had a fight with his daughter, my mum, it would be forgotten.

I took him straight to the bar where I'd seen Alice before. I was hoping we'd find her there. This time I had a reason to go up to her straight. If she was with some bloke, well fine, it wasn't a secret any longer.

We walked in, Herbert following me, and waded through the noise of the place. I couldn't see her, but it was so crowded that it was no wonder.

'I think she's in here somewhere,' I shouted above the noise.

Herbert pointed to a bar up on the first floor and motioned me to go with him. He climbed the stairs. I got the point. She could be up there or else we could spot her more easily if she was down below.

We looked down and I saw her at once.

She was with a man, a geezer with greased black

hair and tight trousers, an Italian-looking bloke with hollow cheeks. He could have been out of a dancing movie, a white hip-hop star. He was the kind of man girls turned their heads to look at.

'Found her,' I said and pointed. Herbert nodded.

Just as we started down the stairs all the lights went on and there were suddenly fifty policemen at the door, pushing their way in.

'There is no need for panic. This is a raid. Can you make your way one by one to any of the exits and leave as quietly as you can. We are sorry to interrupt your evening. On behalf of Leicester Police and the magistrates who signed our warrant, please believe that we have serious reasons for this action. No one is in any danger. Please begin to evacuate the premises.'

There was a roar of anger from the crowd and then a rush to the doors. Herbert and I were swept down the stairs and were then stuck in the crush.

Herbert didn't look comfortable at all. His eyes became shifty. We couldn't go backwards or forwards on our own but were pushed to the door. We were bound to miss Alice.

'I can get through the crowd and grab her,' I said. 'I'll meet you outside.'

I bent low and ducked and dived and got to the other door. I was sure I'd be there before Alice and would grab her.

Before I could find a place to stop, a copper

grabbed me.

'What are you doing here? You're too young to be here. I've got my hands full. So get out of it,' he said and hauled me towards him and out of the door before I could reply.

Outside the door people were hurrying away. I waited for Alice, checking everyone who stepped out. The police were stopping some people and others were led away to police vans. It was a bit chaotic.

After maybe twenty minutes the place was empty but I'd missed Alice. Maybe she had fought her way sideways and left by the other door. Maybe she was still inside.

Herbert would be waiting, so I nipped over to the other door, but I couldn't see him anywhere. I ran up and down the street. No Herbert. He must have pushed off to catch his train.

I felt gutted, man. That was my chance. My one bloody chance. Maybe he'd reckon that I'd go back home and he'd join me there since he'd lost me. I walked back.

I stayed up till two, but Alice never came. Nor did Herbert.

I got into bed with my clothes on and stayed awake. She came back in the morning, but only to pack her stuff.

She looked at me with big, sad eyes. She asked me to sit down, her voice getting husky. I sat down.

'I have to speak to you. I am in trouble. It's best that I leave you, Rashid. You know the Das business, the drugs and all that. The police have caught on and they are after me and I don't want to involve you in any of it.'

'You mean you don't want to involve me with your Italian hip-hop dancer.'

'What are you talking about? Have you been smoking the stuff? Keep reality and fantasy separate.'

'That's funny coming from you, innit, Davinia, or Alice?'

'Why don't you understand? The rent is paid for three months. We've got cash. You can take it all. You can have the computers. I don't want to risk you going down with me. I want to get you out of dealing. And me. Let's talk this over. Keep the phone on. Wherever I am I'll call you in a day or two and then you can join me if it's safe. Maybe we'll talk about finding your mum instead of all this rubbish about Big Top and your grandpappy from the circus. It's possible that the best thing for you is to go back to London and get in touch with the social workers who can't have forgotten you yet.'

I felt like Jesus must have when he heard that Judas had taken cash to grass him.

'The geezer in the pub,' I said, making the connection.

'Why have you been following me?' said Alice. She

paused and then she recovered. 'You shouldn't have followed me. I'll tell you about him. He's a friendly cop.'

'Did they get you in the raid? I was there.'

'Yes, they got me, but they didn't know who I was so they searched me and let me go. It's getting really dangerous, we've got to pack it in. But this fellow, he's the one I've been speaking to – you know, when you got jealous – and he told me that they are after me. He is a plainclothes guy on the drug squad and he came to warn me that I could go down for lots of years. I don't think they'll bother you once I'm gone, Rashid. Will you forgive me?'

It was like she'd punched me in the gut.

'A plainclothes policeman? That fellow?'

'Something like that.'

'And you're on the run?'

'Rashid, I'm sorry. I hate to leave you, but we've got to split up because if they have me, they'll have you, see?'

I could see.

'But I'll settle matters and call you tomorrow.'

'Don't bother,' I said. 'I've got my own plans.'

'No you haven't. I'll call you, but I've got to go off on my own for a day at least. Are you sad I'm leaving?'

I was not going to give her the satisfaction of that one. I was actually gob-smacked and I didn't know why but water was coming into my eyes and I was blinking to make it drain away.

'Don't be sad,' said Alice. 'The whole thing here was crazy.' She kissed me on the forehead and I stepped back. I didn't want her lips or anything anywhere near me.

For a moment she looked as though she was going to change her mind. She was talking to herself in her own mind. Then she says, 'No, it was an illusion. A mirage. You got to face the facts.'

I didn't want to say nothing to that.

She took out all the money we'd got from dealing, a lot of money, and gave it to me.

'It's everything we've got.'

'If you're going to jail you won't be needing it,' I said and took the cash even though I really wanted to throw it in her face.

'Don't follow me. Please. Stay here at least two days and put the phone on. I'll call you and tell you what's going on.'

'From jail?'

'From wherever, Rashid,' she said.

She took the one bag she now had and left.

'You're not Alice,' I shouted after her at the door. 'You're a professional liar.'

Gone. Alice was Daffy again. She said she was on the run from the police. OK. I thought of the rabbit run, where the rabbit thinks running, but it's where it can't.

I waited a day but she didn't call. Then I thought, to hell with her. I'm on my own just like I was before. I had Big Top's card in my pocket and I pulled it out. It had the address.

six

Idecided to go back to Slough. I flogged both the computers at a bargain price to the landlord's brother who came to fix the sink. He was kind. He asked where I'd go and I said I had an uncle in Slough and I was going to meet up with Alice again.

He didn't believe a word of it, but he was nice because he said I could go and live with his family and be like a relative to them. They had an old mum and his brother would welcome me and they'd teach me bits of building and repairs and if I didn't have anyone else, I could be part of their family.

To tell you the truth, I thought about it for a bit. Or a lot. And that's what I had – nothing. At least I'd learn how to fix lead on roofs and how to mend toilets and paint houses and then maybe one day I'd own a house and . . . Nah, it was too boring.

There was another question that bothered me and it wasn't soft or naff, but I was thinking about whether I was in love with Alice. No, not with Alice, with Davinia. I had meant what I shouted. She was a liar, but for the past four months she was all I had. And I

146

didn't want anything else.

As the train passed Market Harborough I was thinking how I would know whether I was in love or not. There isn't a test, is there? Except the person you think you're in love with, you don't want them to belong to no one else and you think of them a lot. The best is that sometimes thinking of the person makes your heart beat faster and if you get the faintest feeling that they fancy you also then you get a ticklish feeling in your stomach. It's hormonical. Love is all to do with hormones. I read that in a women's magazine. It was written by a doctor – no actually by two doctors and they had done this research which said that a little thing at the bottom of your spine started releasing a hormone which then went all over your body and made your blood thinner or thicker or something and then that got connected to whenever you thought of a particular person and made you feel good because your blood was just a bit hotter or something. Then you started connecting the feeling good to that person and images of him or her and that meant you were in love.

At the station in London I saw the papers and read the headlines for free. On the front page of three of them there was a picture of the mad mullah, Abu the beard who had tried to move into my flat. There he was with two geezers on either side of him. The story said he was being arrested for some illegal immigrant

147

racket. I bought the paper. Normally I don't buy them kinda papers, but I had to read this.

Well, I got a place to sit and opened this paper because of Abu the beard who wanted me to go work for him – and there on the third page was a picture of my flat. My flat! Straight up. The photograph was taken from a funny angle. The photographer must have climbed into a corner of the ceiling or something and looked down because he had made the front room and kitchen look huge.

I couldn't believe it. The caption under the photograph said 'The Hideout House'. I read it five times. The police said they were looking for my mum and there it was – a picture of her (with a big feather boa going round the back of her bum). They must have picked it up from the flat. The neighbours and the Council, the bastards, had told the papers her name. They didn't say she'd done anything wrong but they said they wanted to question her. It mentioned me. It said the neighbours thought that 'her son who cannot be named because he's a minor has gone abroad to join his mother.' Then it said, 'The occupants of the flat at Plato House were alleged by the neighbours to have permitted traffic in illegal aliens.'

That would be Hitler and Eva. The neighbours. It was their big day, getting themselves in the papers. And 'illegal aliens', man, like these geezers were from Mars or something. I knew it must have been them that had grassed out of spite, which the papers didn't bother to ascertain.

The police said that Abu the beard or his mates were suspected of regularly shipping in Bangladeshi geezers and putting them to work on the machines making leather jackets and that. Myself, I couldn't see what was wrong with that, but the papers were dead against it. They said they came in by boat and made signals with lamps and got picked up somewhere north and driven down to London to live in my flat.

And now Scotland Yard or whoever had fingered my flat in Hackney something chronic and the papers called it a 'halfway house'. I mean no way my flat was halfway. I went and bought the other papers, all of them, to see what they'd got.

One of them started on about my mum. They said she was known as 'Gypsy'. None of them had a picture of her and none of them mentioned that her real name was Esther, but the journalists had snooped about and talked to everyone on the estate. They had talked. El Rabbito.

But I tell you something, it was funny how little they knew about us. I had always thought that our neighbours were so snoopy that they followed every move we made. But actually they knew nothing. They mentioned my granddad but even though the funeral had gone off from there and the dead body had been moved, no one seemed to have seen it. The police said they'd taken away material to make false passports and stuff. They called it a multi-million pound trade, but I'd seen the geezers involved and they all looked pretty trampish to me, like pathetic.

They also interviewed an international copper who said that they had found the flat through some people in Paris.

They were saying that this was the biggest find on the 'underground railway'. All of them had been taken off to some detention centre and would be packed off home.

Then I got to thinking that it was no big deal. These geezers who came by boat and spent thousands of pounds to get here, they didn't mean any harm, they just wanted jobs and work and some dosh on Fridays, so what was the wretched fuss about? That's how leather jackets get made isn't it? Some of them couldn't speak English, but so what?

Then it struck me that now they'd be looking for me. Maybe they thought I was the chief contact or something, waving lamps at night on the cliffs of Dover or Penzance to signal to the boats. I was searching my head to remember if I had told my address to Alice or to Das, because they would read the papers and they would maybe put two and two together and think I was deceiving them and had run away from an illegal aliens racket, or was still with it and carrying out operations on behalf of the slave traders in Slough and Leicester.

I don't think I had mentioned my place but I definitely had said something to Das about my mum. He knew about me, because I'd blabbed, but I didn't think he'd tell. In fact of all the people I had met, I trusted him most.

Sitting with five newspapers spread across two seats, I must have looked a little strange, like a tramp gathering papers. I reckon I did because people were beginning to stare at me. Kids don't read that many papers.

One old bag was looking hard at me, so I just turned to page three of the paper and started clocking the nude like I was just an ordinary pervert. She came up to me and said, 'You shouldn't be reading that filth at your age. You should be in school.'

'I beg your pardon, that's a picture of my mum you're insulting,' I said. 'She's a model. Beautiful, isn't she?'

I picked up the papers and pushed off, trying to make out I wasn't running.

I wasn't going to go anywhere near Hackney where my neighbours would recognise me and might alert the police. The thought crossed my mind to give myself up. What was it they always said: the innocent have nothing to fear. But it's not true. This drama teacher told us that the cops always pin stuff on you because they can't solve as many crimes as the government wants them to. She got us to do an improvisation which is when you pretend that the copper has stuck some drugs or a knife on you because you're black and minding your own business. This teacher thought she was well hard and some of us had to be bent cops and others had to be the kids who they were stitching up. She used to go dancing in the clubs even though she was a bit old for it, so she thought she was cool.

I had to get out of London and I had a key in my pocket. It was the key Das had given me to his house in Slough.

Sometimes I think there are so many houses and so many beds in the whole wide world and so many keys to so many doors that it's funny that there are some people who have to sleep on the street. I don't mean funny like it makes you laugh, but funny like it makes you cry. And in these magazines, the sort my mum used to read, there were stories about people, girls mostly, being lonely, but that too is a bit funny because if there's the same number of girls and boys, I mean men and women in the world, there ought to be someone in the world for everybody. Adds up, right? It doesn't matter what you are. If you're Chinese and only want a Chinese girl, then there'll be one somewhere in China and if you don't look that good then there's someone else who maybe doesn't look that good either who'll like you.

Except that there's no rule that says the ugly have to go with the ugly. In fact I've seen all sorts of couples when you wonder how they got together, because the women is very tall and the man very short or the other way round, and there are some fat and thin combos and some pretty and ugly combos, but that's a bit rarer from what I've seen.

The train goes from Paddington to Slough. In the films they say they watch all the ports so I looked to see if there were any plainclothes cops on the lookout for me leaving the city. There was a cop but he didn't look interested, and anyway, if the cops were in plainclothes how was I to know who they were? A mate told me that you could always make them out by their shoes, because even when they buy disguises they can't afford to change their shoes, so they always wear those thick black ones, but I don't think that's true any more. The Italian dancer disguise man who picked up Alice, the cop who tipped her off, he was wearing trainers, stylish ones. And apart from being looked for, more scary was the thought that got me as I sat on the train that maybe nobody was looking for me, not even my mum. That's kind of worse than being looked for – not being looked for.

In Slough I walked to Das's place and rang the bell. I still had my things there and I had the key but I didn't want to barge in if he was still in jail. No one answered so I waited a few hours and walked round the place and came back. But there was still no one there and Das's cab wasn't parked outside so I thought he wouldn't mind if I opened the door and went in.

It was dark. I couldn't see a thing. I tried the lights but they wouldn't come on. I went to the kitchen and there was a candle rotting in the corner of the window. I lit it from the gas stove and walked upstairs. I went into the back room where I used to sleep. Believe it or not it still had my clothes and the comics I was reading on the bed. Then I got to Das's room. I was playing detective by candlelight. The room was all over the place. I mean it was there in the same place but it was untidy. Things thrown all over.

I thought I'd give him a surprise and tidy it up, in case he was just out and coming back later, but when I put the candle down and tried to make it stand by leaking wax onto one of his huge loud speakers, it went out. I was in the dark again.

I knew what was wrong. I went to the basement and groped along the wall to find the electric box. Then I threw the biggest switch and the lights in the house came on and as I went up the stairs I could hear music. It was some woman singing:

'*On my own*
Once again . . . '

I waited for Das to come back. I waited three days. I stayed in the house. Most likely he was still away. Or maybe he'd gone to London or wherever to see his mum. On the fourth day a guy came to the door and asked for Das. He was a big man and he was behaving strangely. When I opened the door he put his foot just inside it, as though he was trying to stop me shutting it.

'Where is he then?'

'I don't know.'

'Don't give me that.'

'I really don't know.'

'So who are you then?'

'I . . . I just live here. I'm his relation.'

'When does he get back?'

'I don't know.'

'You don't know anything do you kid?'

'I don't know why I've got to answer your questions for a start,' I said.

'Don't come fresh with me, twerp. I am a bailiff. Your cousin's in deep trouble. I've got ten unpaid parking fines here.' He waved some pieces of paper. 'And I've got a court order right here to take his car and his house and his fridge and maybe even the likes of you with me.'

'I don't think you'll have much luck,' I said. 'Das is in jail. And not for parking offences either. For murder. He killed some fat geezer who came bullying him on this very doorstep. A bailiff, I think he was.'

'Don't give me any lip,' he said. 'I'm doing an

honest job and I didn't get it by reading the bible to little bastards like you. I'll smash your face in.'

'That would not be advisable,' I said. 'You'd lose your job if I took you to court for grievous bodily harm. Then you'd become the tramp you really are.'

I tried to shut the door but he had his foot in it and I just retreated and went to the kitchen and ran out of the back door. I was going to go over the low fence into the alley, because he was well enraged. But he didn't follow me out. He came a few steps into the house and then must have thought he had better things to do because I heard the door slam behind him. I wasn't taking any chances. He might have been smarter than he looked. Perhaps he had walked in and slammed the door behind him, waiting in the hallway for me to think he'd gone and then to wring my neck.

I went over the fence and through the alley and at the corner of the street I saw him in his white van with its wretched 'DEBTOVER SERVICES' sign on the side. He looked angry, with a 'mission unaccomplished' expression on his face. I laughed and let myself in through the front door. Then it struck me: Das might be in jail for ages. How would I find out?

I was thinking about going down to the cab company, even the one run by his enemies and asking them if they knew what had happened to Das. After all, if he was still in jail, they might get a feeling of being sorry for having put a good man down and tell me the story.

I didn't go to the cab services though. I thought better of it. I stayed at home and the next week Mugsy, the bailiff, showed up again, this time with two more blokes. I heard them coming from upstairs and I peeked out of the curtain. They rang and rang but I didn't open the door.

Mugsy shouted through the letterbox.

'We know you're there, twerp, and we know that your man has been put away so let us in. We even know who you are.'

That panicked me. Maybe the other two guys were from Interpol and they had come to get me for the aliens in my flat.

'We have a warrant to break in,' Mugsy was shouting.

I didn't wait to see what they'd do. I picked up the small bag containing my shirt and my dictionary and *Roget's Thesaurus*, like I told you I had left behind at Das's. And I got the rest of it, the Josh placard and the wooden clown and the dumbbell and the tiger tooth and I legged it out of the back window and dropped into the alley and then scrambled over the fence and away into the whole wide world. On my own, once again.

Slough had closed down for me.

And where was I headed? I looked at Big Top's card again. Herbert.

seven

In all this time on the run I had never slept out, slept rough I mean. I tell you, I missed Das. He'd even helped Alice out when she was on the run. Because he had a good heart, man. And these guys, the bailiffs and raiders of other people's stuff, they get away with it when a straight guy, because he deals in the illegal grasses, he gets jugged. It's not fair.

I checked my money. I had what Alice laid on me. But I thought I should save as much as I could. I felt like a squirrel with a bunch of new nuts when I looked at those ten pound notes.

There was the A4 going through the town and I knew it moved west to Reading or somewhere and then maybe Devon was down the road from there. So at a roundabout where a lot of trucks passed, I thought I'd try and hitch a ride.

The cars passed without noticing me. I tried to look the drivers in the eye, but they went past in a flash looking straight ahead or talking to other people in the cars. Only one car stopped with five young men, in it. I was happy they were going to fit me in, so I ran up. The bloke in the front wound down his window and asked, 'Where to mate?'

Before I could answer a boy in the back rolled down his window and spat a stream of brown liquid at me. It fell on my face and down my shirt. They screamed with laughter and pushed off. It smelt like some Cola. I dried my face with the end of my shirt. I felt dirty, sticky with his spit in my face. That's what these pigs are about – being dirty and spreading it.

I stuck my thumb out only when there weren't young guys in the car. Loutish.

At times like these the thesaurus came in useful. I play games with it. Like you find a word and see if you can find the other words that mean the same. For 'story' there's 'tale', right, and I could get that, but for 'permission' there's 'leave' or 'allowance' and I never got those first time, but now I know.

After an hour or more, I waved my thesaurus at a truck and it stopped for me. I ran up and scrambled into the cab.

'Where to, sonny?' the driver asked.

I didn't want to sound as though I didn't know, so I said to the Scilly Isles, because I knew they were in that direction and I didn't want to give him the exact location because later on, if I didn't get on with him, he might grass me and the police would come looking. And anyway, I liked the sound of the Scilly Isles – 'Silly: trivial, foolish, nonsensical.'

'I'm going into Devon,' said the driver, 'so it's good for you, but I'm not taking the motorway. I've got to stop off at small places, so if you're in a hurry you better hop it and try another lorry.'

I couldn't believe my luck. Some mojo was beginning to work in the cosmos. This guy might even be going to the very village.

'No, it's all right. I'm in no hurry. Thanks for stopping.'

There was no chance that I'd hop out again now. I didn't tell the truck driver that I'd been spat at, but I asked for some water and when I thought he was concentrating on his driving I took his bottle and wet my hand with it and got the stickiness off my face. I hate that feeling more than anything. It's like having a dull pain, having sticky fingers or face or sticky anything.

We drove for hours and he started singing songs loudly to himself.

'I always sing,' he said. 'It doesn't bother you does it?'

I couldn't say it did.

Then he said, 'You're an Indian aren't you?'

I didn't want to go into my dad being from Bangladesh and all that, so I said yes I was.

'In that case I want to show you something,' he said and pulled the truck to the side of the road at the next lay-by.

I didn't know what he was going to do, but I was

comfortable with him. 'Vacational, comfy, content, homelike, wealthy and pleased.'

He opened the glove compartment and took out a little jewellery box. Inside it there was a tiny blue stone with one smooth surface, shaped like a little leaf.

'What do you think of that?' the guy asked.

'It's a stone. Pretty,' I said, not wanting to disappoint him. 'Is it worth a lot of money?'

'Priceless,' he said. 'That's a bit of the Taj Mahal, you know. An actual bit of the real building. I pulled it out with my penknife when me and my wife went on a holiday to India. It was part of the carving in the marble so I thought I'd have it as a souvenir. I don't go around scratching my name all over the place you know, like these vandals do, 'Dez luvs Trace' and all that. Much better to have a piece of the original architecture.'

I don't know what the Indians at the Taj Mahal thought of that, but I didn't say nothing.

'It's supposed to be the building where you find love. You know that?'

I said I didn't know.

'And I had a shortage, so I brought it to bring me luck. There's a king buried there. I forget his name. With his wife, like. He wanted to be in the same place. It sounded romantic but I reckon that's what destroyed my marriage. That little bugger there.'

'I'm sorry about that,' I said.

'Yeah, Lucy, that's my wife, came back to England from the Taj Mahal and she couldn't get it out of her head. Every day she'd say to me, when I was at home, because I drive most of the time, why wasn't I building something for her? I said we didn't have the cash and in England people didn't build places like that and she said her friend's husband had spent money on buying a plot in a cemetery where they could both be buried together! Some people buy sofas and new kitchens and holidays; this flippin' gunkhead buys his wife a plot in a cemetery so they can be together. I couldn't get it into her head that we'd spent all our money going to the Taj Mahal and there was none left over to start building one here. But she was like that: once she got a thing into her head she wouldn't let up. She'd go on and on. I tell you she was only twenty two years old and she was already thinking of when she was dead. So I says, 'Think of when you're dead when you're dead, leave it out now,' and she goes that it was the idea of 'not being alone lying side by side' and through all eternity. Some idiot told her that when she was at the Taj Mahal – while I was round the back chivvying this piece out of the wall. I shouldn't have taken my eyes off her because these sharks and lover-boys come round when they see white women and try to sell them something or take them into white slavery. Can't turn your back for a moment in India. Slippery customers.

'You know the Taj Mahal? It's the most beautiful building in the world they reckon and the Indians have just turned it into something commercial. Trying to sell you junk. No offence to you or your family, right, but Indians don't appreciate art, like. It's all money to them.'

'So what did you do in the end?' I asked. 'Did you make her a Taj Mahal?'

He laughed. 'Did I heck?' he said. 'I got fed up of her moaning so one day I bought a big vase and took it home. Here it is,' I said. 'Our own little resting place. I don't believe in burial any more so we'll both be cremated when the time comes and then our ashes can mingle together in the bottom of this flippin' vase. Forever, just like you wanted. Till someone thinks it's a real vase and fills it full of water and your ashes poison the flowers? Satisfied?

'What she replied doesn't bear repeating in young company. It was worse than French.'

He chuckled

'But that was the end. The final Jack Straw.'

We were now off the A roads and moving down some narrowish country lanes.

'I've got to deliver something in the back for a friend,' said the driver.

He turned down a lane and stopped at a farmhouse.

He went in and eight men came out of the farmhouse while I sat in the cab.

'That's my mate. He's an Indian,' he told them.

They opened the back of the truck and untied a grand piano from its moorings. They lifted it down, all black and shiny. A young girl came out of the farmhouse and opened the lid and she began to play the piano.

She was excited. She played something beautiful and all the men listened and I listened and then the men tried to take the piano indoors but they got stuck at the back door of the farmhouse. They hadn't thought of how to get it in. The girl's father came out and he looked and he said the wall would have to go and then be rebuilt. But the girl said she didn't want it in the kitchen. So the father said two more walls would have to go and he'd call a builder the next day. The girl started crying. My driver friend brought the stool out and she sat next to the piano and cried. They were going to demolish the whole house and build it round the piano just because this stupid girl was making a fuss.

We didn't wait. We pushed off. It was getting dark.

After a while we got to where he said he had to head north. He was going back to Bristol on the main road and if I wanted to get to Penzance that night my best bet was to get off where we were. I didn't want to change my story and say I wasn't going to the Scilly

Isles after all. I'd said my mother and stepfather lived there sometimes and I was going to see them and my little sister.

He stopped the lorry at a lay-by and I stepped out. It was dark now.

The truck moved away down the road leaving me alone in the darkness of the countryside at a cross-roads somewhere in Devon. I didn't know where in Devon or how far I needed to go but it was great because I'd get to Herbert and maybe he'd actually tell me straightaway that he knew my grandfather and that old Josh was just down the road. If my mojo in the cosmos held out.

It seemed it was because a car came along and a lady stopped. I almost stepped into the road to make sure she could see me by the single yellow lamp. It was bloody pitch dark. She wanted to know what I was doing. I looked at the sign on the road and read the name of the village. It said Didworthy 6. Herbert's card said Shipley Bottom. So I told the lady that's where I was going.

'At this time of night? Where have you been?' she asked.

'Nowhere, missus, just to a farm where my girlfriend lives.'

'Girlfriend? You have a girlfriend?'

'Just a girl I know from school. I play the piano with her.'

'Piano indeed,' she goes.

She said it was further than she was going but it was out of the way so she'd better take me.

She was in a very posh car which smelled of leather polish and she had an accent which also smelled of leather polish.

She asked me questions all the way and I did what Alice had wanted us to do. I made up a whole life with a family and an uncle and school and a place to live and everything. I even described my dad. I said he was in the army in Germany training people. To most of my answers she said, 'Oh,' as though she'd never heard that sort of thing before. And maybe she hadn't.

And when she dropped me in the village centre, which was all dark and shut down, she said, 'Take care. Now, you do know where you're going?'

'Home, of course,' I said and she said, 'Toodle-oo,' and drove off into the night.

I was tired and hungry now and it was very dark. There were no road lights. There wasn't even a dog in the village and no one on the streets or in the lanes. I wandered around for about ten minutes and came to a church surrounded by a graveyard. There was a broad bench in it so I sat down and soon curled up. Even if I found Herbert's house now, he wouldn't be well pleased. It must be after midnight. I decided I had to hang about and find him in the morning. I took my spare shirt out and covered myself with it

166

and put my bag with my thesaurus and dictionary under my head. They weren't much good, but gave me the feeling that I had made some sort of bed.

I don't think I slept much but I must have because I woke up with an old man leaning over me. I had been dreaming that Mum had come back and we'd gone to the beach together.

It was daylight.

'Dear, dear, dear, right on our doorstep. What have we here?' the old man was saying.

The first thing I saw was a big iron cross dangling over my eyes and when I focused beyond that I saw this thin old man. He was obviously the vicar.

'And where did you come from?' he asked. 'And what did you think you were doing? You could have been eaten by wild animals!' he was joking and laughed at his own joke.

'I didn't mean any harm,' I said. 'I got dropped off here and I was tired.'

'I bet you were. And hungry?'

'I'll move on, sir,' I said.

'Not before you've eaten something, you won't. How long is it since you ate?'

'Day before yesterday,' I said, truthfully.

I'd found noodles and cans in Das's cupboard and I'd been eating those and some eggs and apples I bought.

'Oh dear. You'd better come this way, lad. Food,

food, food.'

I was hungry and I followed him. We went behind the church to the vicar's cottage set within its own stone wall, a sweet little cottage like in the postcards, and he took me through the back door. He didn't have a key or anything, he just lifted the latch on the wooden slatted door and we were in his kitchen.

'What would you like?' he asked

'I don't want to be any trouble, sir.'

'You're no trouble at all. Now come on, eggs and cheese and fruit and cake.'

'Yes, sir,' I said.

He gave me the food that he'd cooked himself and he asked my name. I divulged.

Then he asked what brought me to these parts.

I showed him Herbert's card. 'He invited me. He's got work for me to do.'

The vicar looked at the card. 'You've found the place all right. I'll take you over when you've eaten. Wolf it down.'

After the food we walked to Herbert's place. We crossed several fields and fences. We were onto a moor. And there down in a sort of ditch was Herbert's house.

The vicar rang the bell and, sure enough, Herbert himself came out.

He even remembered my name.

'Crikey!' he said. 'Pardon the Italian. God has

answered my prayers and even sent the vicar to deliver the goods. Rashid, where have you come from. I've been e-mailing Alice frantically.'

'So you know each other. This scallywag was sleeping on the graveyard bench. Tch tch tch.'

The vicar said he had to get on with his work and I thanked him again for the breakfast. He set off back to his cottage.

'You come right in. This is a great surprise,' said Herbert.

'Yes, sir, I'm glad I found you.' What I was dreading now was that he'd ask about the lion tamer's whip and all that and I'd made up my mind to tell him that Alice disappeared with those things, but I had other things like the clown statue.

'And how is your sister?'

'She ran away, sir.'

'I am sorry to hear it. Please do call me Herbert,' he said. 'Or even Hervie. And you've eaten?'

I said I had.

'I've been picking mushrooms. Have to keep myself busy while the museum forms around me.'

He emptied the basket he was carrying on to the table. It contained mushrooms, some twisted, some large, some brown, some white, some like folded umbrellas and some like open ones.

'That's chanterelle and these are little earth stars and you're going to have mushrooms grilled with cheese for supper if you stay. I picked them near the graveyard. Do you like mushrooms?'

And now I looked about me and I could see what he meant by the museum building round him. He had pictures of old circuses and posters that advertised their shows and photographs of lions and horses in cavalcade and trapeze artists in the air stuck up all round the kitchen.

'About the mushrooms,' said Hervie. 'Don't go around picking and eating them. They'll kill you. A few of them are poisonous. You've got to know what you're doing. Now, tell me what happened after the raid, Rashid. Rashid is your name isn't it?'

I told him the truth or as much of it as didn't make me seem crazy. I told him that my mum had gone away to dance to earn money, but not that my grand-dad had moved in on us and then died, or that I had been on the run for a bit because of the Social. I told him I had been with a friend called Das and then I told him that Alice wasn't really my sister.

'I did work that out, you know. She wouldn't be would she? There's no family likeness at all.'

'And that stuff she promised you. She took it,' I said.

'Did she? After what happened I thought it must be a lot of nonsense. Though some of it sounded real. Anyway, there's no memorabilia, no circus stuff?'

'Oh, there is some,' I said. 'I've brought it, right

here in the bag.' I didn't want him kicking me out straight off.

'So you're homeless?' Hervie asked.

I told him I wasn't headed anywhere, and he said I should stay and pick mushrooms. He had three spare rooms in the cottage and was thinking of pickling mushrooms for a living.

'I used to have money, but I squandered it on the circus. Better than drinking or gambling.'

'You mean you went to the circus every day?'

'You're real joker. No, I mean I spent it on circus memorabilia. I bought knick-knacks. I've got a warehouse full of them in Exeter. I just hope the nation will buy them from me and set up a museum. Now, let's have a look at your stuff.'

I showed him the tiger tooth and the wooden clown, but not the note or the dumbbell. I kept those in my clothes bag.

'Oh, I say, that clown's rather splendid. We must find out who did it. It's a portrait obviously. But of whom? I have the real faces of clowns, a whole collection of them. We can look through them together. Please be my guest.'

I said I would like to stay for a bit.

'That's brill,' said Hervie.

He showed me round the house. The top of the house had an attic room which I would sleep in and next to it was a room full of old statues of clowns, golden saddles, chests full of circus costumes and hundreds more posters and prints like the ones I had seen downstairs. He kept that room locked. Then, on the first floor, he had a dark room for photography and another tiny room next to it like a box room in which he had microscopes and experiment dishes and a tiny sink with a boiler for hot water on the wall. There were shelves with bottles of chemicals on them.

'That's the science, now the arts,' he said. His front room had pictures of mushrooms which he had painted himself.

There were several sketches in pencil and in crayon and four very small and delicate portraits in paint of young circus performers.

Some of them were in tights like acrobats and others were men dressed as wrestlers and one young man was clad in a lion skin, just like I imagined my grandfather.

'Is that you?' I asked.

'Dear God, no, that's one of my boys. Gone now. All gone.'

'Your sons?'

'Friends. Boys I used to teach.'

'How old are they now?'

'Let's see, that one over there, Philip, he was a boy acrobat. Gymnast of the first order. Gave it all up. Must be thirty. He has two children of his own.'

'And you are like their granddad?'

'I would be if he brought them to see me. But the truth is their mother doesn't like me and they live far away in East Anglia. I send him a postcard on his birthday but he doesn't reply.'

'Maybe you're sending it to the wrong address. People move on, don't they?' I said because he looked sad when he said they didn't reply.

'No it's not that. He sends them back with 'Not known at this address' clearly written on the envelope and it's always in his own handwriting. I would know that handwriting anywhere.'

'But you still keep sending them?'

'I do.'

'You should try e-mail,' I said, not knowing how to carry the conversation any further.

He realised that and took me to the shed outside which he had made into a cosy room where he made his mushroom pickles. Again, there were jars and containers and trays of mushrooms drying under special lamps, scales and a shining row of knives and scissors which he said were for 'skinning'.

Hervie said he had retired to Devon now but he had taught Botany in London and France and in Liberia and now he'd given that up. He only wanted to take photographs of rare English mushrooms and send them to the botanical magazines and science journals.

He was doing studies of these rare mushrooms at different stages of growth.

'So if you're going to stay anyway, Rashid, I can put you to work on the circus papers. Putting all the names and dates in registers. Just sorting out the featured people from the posters you saw up there for a start. And of course we must get you some clothes and we must find your mother for you. If that suits you, old man.'

He was being kind. I said it would be OK for a while and he nodded.

Hervie had bags under his eyes like some old dog and his skin hung on his jaws. He had a forehead which looked massive because of his knob of a head. I wanted to ask him if that was why he called himself Big Top, but I didn't.

His face was wrinkled, with lines like I hadn't seen before, like the marks one sees on pictures of the planet Mars.

I went up to my attic bedroom and in the night, that first night and then again every night after, I heard him coughing. Hervie gave me a very cosy bed with two blankets. The sloping roof, the sound of the trees outside the window and the birds in the morning made me feel like I was in a dream, like in the good part of a Walt Disney video.

He shouted at me to come for tea in the morning,

early morning, and I didn't want to seem lazy so I got up and dragged my clothes on and went downstairs.

'I woke you up early because that's the rule of the household and because we are going to see what the dew is doing to the mushrooms – to the *Lactarius torminosus* of which I have found a patch,' Hervie explained.

We were out for three hours with cameras and two baskets, each of us looking like Red Riding Hood. He would make me hold one camera and the leather bag of lenses and he would lie on the ground in his over-alls and click the flicks. The vicar came by, muttered a good morning and stopped to ask why I was still there.

'Rashid has accepted the post as my new assistant,' said Hervie

'Good Muslim name,' said the vicar. 'Ass salaam aleikum.'

'Aleikum salaam,' I said.

'I don't know your story or where you come from but I know Hervie will make you feel welcome,' the vicar said and hurried off to open his church.

After lunch Hervie got two trunks of clothes out and opened them up. He showed me the jeans, shirts, T-shirts and stuff he kept in them. It was all good clobber, with great labels, all of them, and some of them were my size.

'They are not your old clothes.' I said. 'These are

brand new, man.'

'I should think they are. Old clothes are for scare-crows.'

He held the trousers and shirts up against me.

'Very fetching, a good match. Try these on. And these . . . and you should try these. They may be a bit large but roll the bottoms up and you'll grow into them.'

'Are you sure I can borrow them?' I asked.

'You are not borrowing them, my dear boy, they are yours. You have been of service and shall continue to be. I shall take it out of your first wages when you work, so don't be too grateful.'

I wanted to ask him why he had these boys' clothes.

'Did they belong to Philip and people like that?'

'No. Philip was long ago. As you remarked, they are fresh and new and let's just say I expected that people your size, or a little smaller or a little larger would come along. And no doubt they will, no doubt they will. You see Rashid I don't expect to stay friendless.'

I tried them on and they did fit and Hervie, who received me in my new clothes in the kitchen, was delighted.

'Do turn round, let's have a look at you. Very fetch-ing, very fit.'

Hervie taught me to pick mushrooms and not get the

poisonous ones when we were foraging, as he used to say, for food.

'The rule, as far as you're concerned, is that there are some varieties we can eat and the rest are poisonous. These mushrooms, some of them are hundreds of years old and the ones next to them, which look just the same, can be a few days old. That's the beauty of them.'

We used to go into the forest and look for Honey Agaric and Chanterelle. They were easy to spot. Even so I must have made a mistake because I was very sick that night.

Hervie looked after me, made me a mixture of hot water and spice which set my stomach OK again.

'I learnt all this when I was a senior scout,' he said.

Hervie had been a scoutmaster in his time and a teacher and explorer. He had once been an archaeologist and had dug up graves. He said he found some of the most interesting mushrooms growing in or near old tombs. He brought out old photographs of himself as an explorer, next to a dead guy in a rotting box.

'The point is that the skeleton is still perfectly formed,' Hervie said.

He had photographs of everything he'd done and was very proud of them. There were hundreds of pictures of young men on the trapeze, of young fire-eaters and jugglers and a few of clowns.

As he leafed through his albums he would mention

the names of the boys with whom he was pictured. There was Richard from the school in which he taught and there was Abu the elephant boy, a circus lad, Geraint the magician, Phedus the equestrian artist, James and John the acrobats and Philip the gymnast of course, and others who kept recurring.

'Some of them you only met when the circus came to town?' I asked.

Hervie didn't reply at first. Then he said:

''Tis all a chequer board of nights and days
Where destiny with boys for pieces plays
Moves hither and thither and mates and slays
And one by one back in the closet lays.'

There was something sad about Hervie when he talked like that. He was thinking something very deep, digging into memories.

That's what struck me about him right from the off. He was a geezer living in the past in his own head and he wouldn't even talk about it. Like he had taps marked 'past' and 'present' and the one marked past was tightly shut and there were only drips coming out of it.

'And what was your connection with the clown's statue?' he asked.

'It was given to my grandfather,' I said. 'By a friend.'

'Good piece. Very fine.'

'I think the clown made it himself,' I added.

'More than likely,' he said. 'Such talented boys, dedicated to laughter.'

A week passed and we went down by the village bus to Buckfastleigh and then on another bus to Exeter.

In Exeter Hervie took me to his treasure trove, the warehouse where his circus museum pieces were stored.

It was a bit of a wonder. An old shed among a lot of sheds, but without cracks and well secure.

There were hundreds of things: chariots, magic props, mazes for animals, wooden cages with trap doors, hundreds of costumes on dummies, spotlights, paintings of big tops and stuffed animals – lions and bears with rings in their noses, some stunt bikes, an old antique car used by clowns and two motorbikes with twisty handles, clubs for juggling, trapezes and traps.

Herbert was proud of it.

'That's Big Top's collection, and I'll tell you a secret, nobody cares, not really. I'll need millions to get this lot going.'

A sadness again crept into his voice.

On the way back he made me carry another load of posters and he himself carried a large multicoloured circus ball which seals used to balance on their noses and spin.

When we got to his village and walked the last mile to the cottage in the ditch, I fetched the dumbbell and showed it to him. He couldn't believe his eyes.

'I know some of the names,' he says. 'Not personally, but by reputation. 'Brazzio Brazzi', big time, my my. Can we do better than that?'

'I one Fabio Romani,' I said.

He didn't bat an eyelid.

'Marie Correlli, *Vendetta*,' he said. He knew the name of the writer and the book, just like that, from one sentence. 'And you've got it wrong. The actual words are...' and he told me, but I've forgotten because once you learn a line one way, you can't forget it and learn it a new way.

Hervie never came into my room in the attic, except to help me change the bed. He'd come up with clean sheets and then he'd just start changing them.

So that was the life there. He'd get the newspapers every day and read them at breakfast. I used to read them too, for the sports pages even though I didn't support a team, and to see whether there was anything more about my flat or about Abu the beard or the aliens or about my mum.

There never was, but Hervie was quite impressed that I looked through the newspapers.

'I don't know many boys who'd do that, Rashid,' he would always say.

'I keep hoping for the comics, but there never are

any,' I said.

'There was an ad for a nineteenth century lion-tamer's kit. I phoned the chap up,' Hervie added.

'What do you want that for? What is it? A whip and chair?'

Hervie ignored that.

'He was very vulgar. He said he wanted four hundred pounds for the whip. He said, "That's the bottom line." For a bottom line that's over the top,' Hervie said.

The village near Hervie's cottage was tiny and I thought of it now as my village. It kind of became my home for a bit. Months actually. Our cottage was some way from it and he'd send me down to the one shop in the village to get some more eggs or to give someone apples or mushrooms or gooseberries that grew in our garden. No one asked me why I wasn't at school. There wasn't a school nearby. Not one for kids more than eleven.

Now and then Hervie would get very concerned about my mum and the rest.

'We must find your mother. Why don't you phone home in London and see if she's back? Aren't you worried by it? I am very happy and flattered to have you here, Hervie's little helper, but if she returns and finds you missing, she'll go to the police.'

I didn't know how to explain to him that she wouldn't have returned, so I told him lies.

'She's not coming back for three years. She has a three-year contract for dancing at this club in Israel.'

'But you do know the address of the club? So we can write to her and tell her you're safe?'

I was sure that Mum would be writing to London and expecting me to write and call, but the last thing I had was one postcard with an address in Tel Aviv which I'd tucked into the thesaurus.

I began work on the posters in the attic, taking down all the names of the people that appeared on them: the names of the clowns, all the Popos and Cocos and Madam Har de Har. There were a hundred people called 'The Great this' or 'The Astounding that' but no mention of The Great Josh Rabbit.

I had to take all the names down on lists on the computer.

'It's slow work, it'll take you years. We must bring in help,' Hervie said.

He had a bike in the shed which he brought out and showed me. It was a fussy bike, a big heavy one, but he'd kept it real clean. It had a basket and a pillion seat at the back with a spring to put shopping on and a little leather case with tools and a puncture kit strapped to the underside of the cross bar. It even had a pump that fitted on to two hooks on the frame.

'It's fully equipped,' Hervie said. 'I'm getting too

old for it, but it's yours when you want to get out and about, into the village and beyond.'

The bike was good. I sometimes got fed up of Hervie and I began to go around the countryside on it. Apart from doing Hervie's mushroom things and doing my poster work, there was not much to do. Then Hervie told me that about ten miles away there was an old stately home with stables and an open swimming pool which the local lads used and now that the days were getting hot, I should cycle there and check it out.

I thought it was a great idea and I went. I found the place. It was like a castle with a long drive with trees on either side and it was in a bit of a state. The swimming pool wasn't much either. It was a big stone pond, which the geezer who looked after it said was built two hundred years ago.

The water was a bit slimy and green but a lot of people came to swim there.

I went to the pool a few times and minded my own business. I'd swim and then eat the sandwiches Hervie always made and packed for me, and then cycle home. The people who came there called it The Lido. On hot days it got quite crowded.

I met this black kid called Anson there. He used to come from the town and he got talking to me because he was one of the few people who came there by bike and one day I saw him walking away from the place wheeling his bike. We'd been fooling about in the pool together and he'd said he lived in town where there were other swimming pools with facilities and that, but he liked biking out here on his own.

'Got a puncture,' he said as I was going past down the long tree-lined drive. He had a smart bike too and I was kinda ashamed of the solid old-fashioned one that Hervie had stuck me with. Alone with it, I was fine, because it had all the gear and stuff, but when it was in the company of other bikes, like real mountain and speed jobs, it was like having a dirty mongrel at a dog show or wearing bombers for PE when the other kids had *Nikes*.

'I can fix that,' I said. 'I got a kit here.' For the first time I wasn't ashamed of the thunderer.

'That's a real phew!' Anson said. 'I thought I was going to have to walk back to town.'

We got the tools out, parked the bikes against a tree and fixed his puncture and pumped his wheel up again.

He was well relieved and we agreed to meet up again at the Lido in three days time.

We got talking a lot. I suppose with all the other blokes coming from Devon and Anson being from Wales, from Cardiff, we got along better. It was like we understood each other. The thing was that he had family trouble and he didn't care to say what, but it had resulted in him being put under a care order and now he lived in town in a care hostel which sounded a bit like Lemon Grove. I didn't want to tell him that I'd run away from one myself or anything more about Lemon Grove and Delilah but I think he guessed that I was on the move in some way, from the hood, not the 'burbs.

I told Anson I was working for Hervie and a bit about the circus stuff we had stored in the cottage and also that I was on a kind of detective search, trying to track down my grandfather. He got well interested in that. He wanted to be a film-maker and go to film school, he said, and his heroes were Eddie Murphy and the Simpsons on telly.

I said I knew how to develop and print photographs in the dark room and he got well hooked on that too. He said he wished he could try his hand at that and I said he was welcome whenever he could get a day off.

He just laughed at that. He said the kids in his home went to school when they felt like it. They could escape and even stay the night out.

'If we walk out the door, they can't stop us. The workers have to let us go,' he said. 'If they try and use physical restraint, that's assault and we can have them.'

'I know that,' I said. 'I passed through one of them myself.'

That just slipped out, but he already suspected, I guess, and he didn't want to go into it. He was more legalistic.

'What you got to avoid is getting into any scrap

with them. If you try any physicals, like push them or even push past the workers then they get entitled, man. They can hang on to you and use restraint and that's it. They can then lock you up and say it's answering violence. They can't touch you till you touch them, right?'

'Yeah, I get it,' I said. 'They can't initiate.' The thought crossed my mind that I could tell him about Frankie and how I'd beaten him up, but I forebore.

One morning Anson came to the cottage. He said he'd told the workers he was off and he'd spend a couple of days there, see how it went.

Hervie was very hospitable. When I cycled up with Anson he kind of bent over backwards to accommodate him and stirred up some fantastic food.

'Your friend arrives at the right time,' Hervie said. 'I've got a surprise for you.'

'Beer?'

'No, significant stuff. Fortune smiles. Come and see.'

In the room that Hervie used to call his 'parlour' there was a mess of brown paper and sticky tape on the carpet and a pile of posters which had been sent to him by post.

'More work,' I said.

Anson was watching.

'And this,' said Hervie and he pulled out a poster that he'd taken out of the pile.

It was a large poster and it said 'THE COSMO CIRCUS' and there on the left, down the side among the list of attractions for this circus was the name 'JOSH RABBIT, THE CHALLENGING STRONGMAN'.

I had to sit down.

'Take it in, take it in,' said Hervie. 'We're on track. And no worries, I've been on the phone and on the Internet and made my enquiries. The Cosmo Circus is no more, but in a few days we shall have contacts who can tell us where it dispersed. You see circus people don't just disappear, they move on to the next circus. That's the beauty of it. They don't settle down and open greengrocer's shops, they ramble on till someone wants to see what they've got to show. So, let's keep tracking, man, as you would say.'

'That's not what I'd say,' I said. 'But thanks. Oh, wow, Hervie, you done it.'

'Not yet, but this trail might lead us, to Josh himself, Allah willing.'

'Josh Rabbit is my grandfather,' I said for Anson's benefit, and I gave Hervie a hug. 'Thanks man, that's purely unexpected.'

'My pleasure. I was taken aback myself. Cosmo's was still going in the early seventies and then it packed up.'

I didn't want to get Anson involved with all this internal talk, so I told Hervie that he wanted to see the dark room.

'I'll give him the whole guided tour,' Hervie said. 'But later.'

After lunch Hervie spent hours in the dark room with Anson, teaching him the lot. We then went out and shot some photographs of mushrooms and when Anson fell over in the mud, we took photos of his mucky face and hands and clothes. After we got back, Hervie and Anson went into the dark room and made different sized prints of all that. I was left with the posters.

I took down the names of all the other acts advertised on the poster for The Cosmo Circus and compared them to the names on the dumbbell. There was only one name that was the same: Stanislav the clown. That was heavy, man. Both of them on the same poster. What did Mum know about Stanislav?

Anson stayed in the cottage that night and Hervie lit a fire after dinner and we sat around and he gave us brandy to drink and told us stories about the circus people he knew and how he had first met them when he was a scientist dealing with plants and animals in Africa and the trappers had come to pick up some wildies.

The next morning Anson and Hervie went off again to take more photographs and then came back in the afternoon and developed them. They seemed to get on good. I didn't go with them because I wanted Hervie to follow the lead we'd got and get down to finding Josh, but he only said that he'd already put out feelers and would wait a few days for the feedback.

'You mustn't start jumping the gun, old man. We will move slowly but surely. There's a little tracker I've put on your Josh's trail right now.'

Anson stayed another night with us and again Hervie made us a great dinner. Next morning Anson left for town. He said he had to report back, but he'd phone and get back to us just as soon as he could get away. Hervie said he was sad to see him go, but when Anson had gone I pestered him to get on the phone and check his contacts, the tracker bloke. I looked two times through the other posters to see if any of the people on the dumbbell were on them, but they weren't.

I looked at the statue of Stanislav. He'd painted it with a kind of transparent red paint, not thick, but like a jelly you could see through and under the red paint on his jaw and neck you could see the carved wrinkles. And under his eyes, under the white paint which I only now noticed was just as transparent, you could see through, to a web on the skin. That was weird. What was Stanislav giving this to Josh for?

I brought the note out now. It was the last thing I had hidden from Hervie. The note which was maybe written by Stanislav and said:

For Josh,
Be luckier than old Stanislav.
My face, my life, my sorrow.

I showed it to Hervie and he sat down and thought about it, clutching the yellow paper in his hand.

'My face, my life, my sorrow,' he repeated – and then, 'Oh, my gosh, we have stumbled on a story here.'

I could have told him that weeks before, but now he saw it. A story. Josh and Stanislav.

'Josh and Stanislav,' Hervie muttered to himself. Josh and Stanislav.'

Anson came back two days later. He just biked back and said he wanted to be with Hervie and me for a day or two and not to worry, he had permission.

'So why are you back?' Hervie asked him.

'Because this is the place, man. I gotta make more photos.'

In three days he reckoned he knew a whole heap about photography, and it was true that he made large prints of a lot of things – mostly the mushrooms and some of Anson himself posing. He loved the attention, I reckon, because Hervie always treated both of us like we were adults. No nonsense.

Hervie knew that I was getting shifty about finding Josh, so he says, 'Look Rashid, I know hundreds of circus people. I've got to them through the Net and

I've asked them to tell me anything they know about Josh or Stanislav. Just cool it.'

I couldn't cool it. I asked him if I could check his e-mails every few hours and he said, 'Be my guest and damn the rest, 'cause you're the best.'

'That's childish, Hervie,' Anson said.

'One reverts,' says Hervie.

So when they go out, I check the e-mails and one of them says:

Stanislav the clown? Sure, sure. Dead. Murdered.

The person who sent this message to Hervie had a funny name that I hadn't heard before: Cassandra.

I left the message on screen and went down the stairs to the dark room to tell Hervie about it. But I stopped. On the stairs.

There were arguments, man. Goings on between Hervie and Anson. It just took two seconds, then there were smashing noises and Anson ran down and out of the door.

I followed him down, shouting his name. But he didn't stop. He was screaming things, man, I couldn't hear what. He ran to his bike. It was evening, but not yet dark and as I rushed out of the house I just caught Anson getting on his bike and pushing off.

'Anson man, hold on,' I shouted. Or something like that.

I couldn't catch his reply, but it sounded vicious.

I went back into the kitchen and Hervie came down

191

looking pale.

'What happened to Anson?' I asked.

'He's a stupid boy,' Hervie said and he put his hand on my shoulder. 'He . . . I think he misunderstood. But that's absurd. He's a reasonable guy, he'll be back. He'll come back tomorrow and then we'll cook him a delicious meal.'

Hervie did cook a delicious meal of pheasant in apple sauce and cream and there was a lot of it, enough for three Ansons but he didn't come. Throughout dinner I could see that Hervie was listening out for the whirr of his bike. It never came.

That night Hervie did a funny thing. I woke up in the middle of the night because I felt that my face was being stroked by light. I don't know if it's possible but I sometimes feel as if bright light gets through my eyelids, and even though my eyes are shut I know that the light's there. Like looking at the sun with your eyes shut and seeing orange. Anyway, I opened my eyes to find a torch flashing right in my face. It was Hervie and he didn't expect me to wake up.

'Er . . . Are you all right?' said Hervie. 'I heard you talking in your sleep. But obviously you're fine.'

He was hasty about leaving, damn quick, but I still saw that he had one of his cameras in one hand and the torch slung around a tape on his neck.

'I was downstairs doing some work and I heard you

talking. You do chatter in your sleep, Rashid, and it gets me.'

'I didn't know that. But why didn't you turn the light on?'

'Oh, I was in the dark room, you know, and I had the torch. But it doesn't matter now. I'll turn in too. Good-night. Sleep tight.'

I didn't fall asleep straightaway. I was sure that Hervie had been taking pictures of me when I was asleep. That was strange.

In all the weeks I had stayed there, I had never actually been into Hervie's bedroom. I passed it on the landing and he always left his door ajar.

But that business bugged me.

'What happened to Anson?' I asked the next morning.

'I told you. Stupid misunderstanding. He's a city boy, streetwise with a vivid imagination. But he'll think it out as it really was, every move and then he'll be back,' Hervie said. 'He likes us and depends on us.' He'd been thinking about it, too, worrying about it.

Hervie went off on the bus the next day. I didn't know for sure because he said nothing to me, but I think he was going to town looking for Anson.

I went into the dark room and pulled the shades up. The developer had been smashed and Hervie must have swept the smashed bits under the table to hide them. The chemical bottles were broken and Hervie had swept up the glass and piled it for removal.

I maybe shouldn't have, but I went into Hervie's room. It was as I expected, perfectly neat with a large double bed and huge pillows. There was a writing table and on all the walls there were sketches and photographs of boys. Some of them were the same boys as downstairs drawn in what I could now easily recognise as Hervie's style. I listened a second for footsteps to see if he was coming back and then I opened the drawers of the antique writing table. In the drawers there were loads of plastic boxes, blue, yellow and red. I pulled one out. It was filled with photographs. They were all photographs of boys. Nothing bad, just boys in swimming trunks and having showers. Photographs.

I knew I shouldn't have looked. I put the boxes away and quickly shut the drawers and went downstairs again, making sure that I hadn't disturbed anything.

Hervie came back late that evening and didn't say where he'd been. I was desperate to ask him – what had Anson been shouting about?

I didn't let on to Hervie that I knew his secret. I didn't even know if it was a secret and whether he'd mind me knowing. Maybe he was going to show me them photographs himself one day when he was sure that I wouldn't take it the wrong way and think he was a pervert or something. But that's what kept going round in my head: Hervie the Pervie, Herv the Perv. I was really wondering whether I should tell him that I'd seen the pictures and find out what he'd say, or whether I should just sneak off and make my way to somewhere else. Go on the run again.

'Where did you go, Herv?' I asked. I thought it was time to cheer him up.

'I wanted to see Anson. I think he made a mistake. Or maybe I made a mistake.'

And just as he was saying that, a car drove up. Two people got out, a man and a woman, and they rang the bell, pulling the rope.

'I'd better get it,' said Hervie. 'I don't like the look of this and it may turn ugly. Will you go upstairs. Please. I'd rather you didn't hear this.'

I nodded and went upstairs but I could still hear it. The house was as still as a pyramid.

'Mr Astley, I'm Roseanne and this is Greg from Devonshire Social Services. A young man called Anson has been visiting you.'

Hervie calls them in and shuts the door of the parlour hoping I won't hear.

Roseanne says that Anson went back to the care hostel and told the workers that Hervie had touched him up in the dark room.

I couldn't hear what they were saying beyond that, but the two visitors soon left and Hervie sat by his fire. I went down to talk to him.

'What did they want?' I asked.

'Your friend Anson has been telling lies about me,' he said.

He was crying, and the worst was that through his tears he looked scared. 'Ugly. Monstrous.'

Hervie repeated the words. He seemed broken.

'Are you going to go on the run?' I asked.

'I have nowhere to go. I haven't done anything wrong. I don't know what Anson is talking about. I bent down to look in his face and he misunderstood. I thought we were mates.'

I didn't know what to say to that. I went upstairs after a bit.

Hervie sat till morning in the parlour, adding log upon log to the fire.

In the morning I found him there.

'Shall I make you some tea?'

Hervie said, 'Do you know about the photographs?'

I said I did. He didn't ask me how.

'They are straightforward photographs,' he insisted. I never did anything wrong. I might have felt things, but if I did I kept them in control. I never harmed anyone.'

He just sat there silent, swallowing, looking into the distance. As I looked at him I thought the flesh on his face was melting, like ice-cream in the heat.

In the evening he said he wanted me to help him.

He went upstairs and brought down all the plastic boxes of photographs and we took them into the woods with some spirit from his pickling shed and we set fire to the lot. Hervie cried as he lit the match. He didn't burst into big sobs, but the tears trickled down his pitted cheeks. We watched and smelt the pictures go up in flames.

I tried to get to sleep but came down when I heard Hervie removing all the pictures from the living room. I got into the act and helped. He held the portrait he'd painted of the boy Philip for a long time.

He became silent. Almost totally silent. He didn't want to deal with mushrooms or gather them or go into the dark room. He read the papers and he went for walks and I went with him but we walked almost in silence. His movements had slowed down.

Sometimes he'd point out how one could tell the age of a tree, or he'd fiddle with a sapling and take the weeds off it. But he said very little. Even the food he cooked was simple. He stopped showing off with it.

A week after the social workers come around, the newspapers had a front page story about some pervert who'd kidnapped a little girl. It had nothing to do with us, or him.

The story lasted ten days. Every day Hervie would send me out to buy the papers. He was sad about the story. He didn't even want to face the village shopkeeper himself and he asked me if I minded biking it eight miles to the next village where there was a larger shop. I knew my way across the hills and fields and it wasn't that long through the woods. I'd go and get the *Sun* and the *Mirror* for him. The man who had kidnapped the little girl must have killed her because she was found dead and there were headlines and front pages in black. We didn't have any telly but I can imagine the telly must have gone wild on it.

Hervie was very touchy.

'I've never been to prison, Rashid,' he said.

I didn't know why he was saying that.

'They tried to make out that I was a pervert and they took me to court. The boy scout troop and the police. But I hadn't done anything. They couldn't find me guilty of anything.'

After a while he said, 'Rashid, do you believe me?'

I said, 'Yes. Except about Anson. I knew the guy, man, and you tried to touch him up in the dark room. What do you expect?'

He was quiet and swallowed hard. He looked like a dog who'd been beaten.

Then I said, 'Look man, I brought Anson to you as a friend, and you took advantage.'

'No advantage. I made friends. Maybe I took too close an interest,' he said. 'For beauty. I have been an apostle of the Muses. No, not an apostle, a wretched captive.'

God may have forgiven Hervie, but people didn't. The vicar called the next day and told Hervie that he'd had complaints from the villagers that there was a pervert in the village. They had even said it was him. The villagers said he was living with a boy, with me. I was listening to all this.

'He's not living with no boy, it's me. You brought me here yourself, remember?' I said to the vicar.

'Yes, of course, and yes, you are living here. I believe you, but . . . ' the vicar was scared. He told Hervie that maybe he should come along on Sunday after the church service and talk to some people from the village. The vicar said there may have been some misunderstanding. The village mechanic's wife who worked with the psychological disorders unit in the town had been in touch with social workers who had mentioned his name. The vicar said he knew Hervie and was confident he wouldn't hurt a mushroom.

Then about fifteen cars came down from the town and fifty very rough people came out of the cars and stood outside Hervie's house and started shouting against perverts and people who murder children. They were low-life people. Not London low-life, like I was used to with Hitler and Eva, but country low-life with a couple of Rottweiler dogs and everything. Hervie drew the curtains and asked me to stay in the attic and not to show my face. The people with placards didn't go away till that evening.

Then two coppers came to the door with the vicar and they spoke to Hervie. He called me down and said he was packing his things because the police were taking him away.

'For what?' I asked. 'He hasn't done nothing?'

The police looked at me in a funny way. I could see them thinking that I was his boyfriend or something.

'For his own protection. And yours. What are you doing living with him anyway. Are you related?' one policeman said.

The other one told him to shut up. All that could wait.

'We can't leave you here either, son,' he said. 'There are some nasty people out there.'

'You'd better come with us,' Hervie said. 'We can come back when all this clears up. I shall phone your mother in the States and tell her that we are both fine and going for a short holiday to Exeter.' He turned to the cops. 'The boy is staying with me. He's my second cousin's son.'

The police drove us to Exeter. There were photographers outside the police station and they took pictures of Hervie, but when one tried to take pictures of me, one of the coppers told him not to. And when he kept doing it, the cop gave the photographer a smart karate blow on his wrist and made him drop his camera, just to show him who was boss.

'I said "no," Rover,' the policeman said. I'd never heard a policeman being funny before.

It was the same cop who sat me down and asked me what I was doing with Hervie. I had taken Hervie's hint and I said my mother was his cousin and because she had business in the States, I was living with him in the holidays.

He wasn't bothered about who I was and he started asking me about what Hervie had done to me. Did he touch me? Did he try and look at me in the bath? Did he photograph me? Had he ever suggested that I sleep in his bed or he sleep in my bed?

I said no to all of that. Because that was the truth. Then he asked if I'd burnt some photographs in the woods with Hervie. I hesitated.

'It's not a crime,' he said. 'It wasn't evidence at the time.'

I felt I was betraying my friend. I got a knot in my stomach and then a light feeling, a butterfly in the stomach, like the girls' magazine said you get when you're in love. But this was because I was grassing him up. I said yes, we'd burnt some photographs.

'They don't burn very well. What were they?'

I told him what I knew of the photographs. He took notes.

'And the boy Anson, you picked him up at the Lido?'

I knew from the way he was asking that it was a trick.

'Anson is my mate,' I said.

'Yes, a good mate. So you took him to Herbert's house and introduced him to Herbert.'

'That is correct,' I said, because that's what you say to policemen.

'And he became friends?'

'Yep.'

'And then Herbert touched him up in the dark room?'

'I wasn't there.'

'You heard a commotion?'

'I heard some noise, but I don't know what.'

'You don't know what? Good, but it was you who brought Anson to Herbert. You can see what I am getting at, Rashid.'

'I can't,' I said and that was the truth.

'You know Anson has complained,' he said

'Not about me, he hasn't,' I said.

'I don't know what exactly he did say. But tell me, did Herbert ask you to bring Anson to him?'

'No.'

I knew where he was going so I decided to say no to everything.

'Did Herbert touch Anson while you were looking?'

'No.'

'And you saw the dark room after Anson ran away. Was it disturbed? Smashed up?'

'No.'

'Is Herbert a pervert, Rashid? Come on, lad, you can tell us. You made friends with Anson and in all innocence you invited him back where you were living. You were not to know that this was going to happen.'

'Don't know,' I said

'Come on, Rashid. We want nothing from you but the truth. If your friend Hervie is dangerous we're going to put him away. If he's not and he's done nothing wrong, he's as free as the wind.'

'And me?'

'Oh you? We want nothing with you.'

'Then why are you taking down what I say?'

'Photographs, Anson. Groping, feeling him up . . . it might all add up.'

The phone rang in the room and he answered it and left, saying he'd be back in ten minutes. He left the door open. Had I betrayed Hervie? Had I talked too much?

I went to the door. I walked down the corridor and passed two lady coppers. I asked them where the water was and one of them said in the foyer, in a machine.

I walked to the foyer and out into the evening. What was I going to do about Josh and Stanislav and the leads that Hervie had got hold of? I was on my way to the railway station when a cop car drew up by me and the same policeman who had interviewed me got out.

'You in a hurry, Rashid?'

'Thought I'd get a bit of fresh air,' I replied.

'Look, I have to tell you that we're not charging you yet, so we can't keep you without your parents being present. I'm just asking as a friend if you want to come back to the station and talk. You don't have to.'

The stuff about parents scared me. They might look into my records or something and find Frankie? The men in my flat? The Social in London? Did they know I knew Das and Alice?

'I want to talk to Herbert,' I said.

I got in the cop car and they took me to another station and walked me from the back yard to the cell where they had seated Herbert.

They let me loose in the cell and I looked around. It was just a room, but there must have been cameras in it or something.

'Have they treated you well?' Hervie asked. He looked tired and suddenly younger, like a guy in prison in a film.

'Yeah,' I said. 'And I never grassed you or nothing.'

'Oh, I know you wouldn't. This is a mess. And they're serious. They're trying to pin stuff on me that won't hold water. Unlike Pampers.'

He managed a smile.

'They're not getting very far with me,' he added. 'In the end there's nothing to hide. Still, I want you to walk away from it. Forget you ever met me.'

'I can't do that.'

'Try.'

The door opened and the policeman brought in a bloke with a briefcase. A tall man with a fur-collared coat.

'That's Andrew, my solicitor,' Hervie said. 'Look, Rashid. Here, I've written down stuff you want to know. Josh Rabbit, real name Josh Rabinovitch, is alive and healthy. Your grandfather. Maybe I should have told you earlier.'

So Hervie knew and he'd been holding out. He must have seen the thought cross my mind.

'I didn't want you to leave, so I kept the information. I must confess, I have known for some time and it's not good news. Though it may be. Your grandfather is in an open prison in Scotland serving a life sentence. He was convicted of murder. He's got two years more, so he'll come out soon. He says he's innocent. To this day.'

'Who did he kill?' I asked.

'His friend. I wish I didn't have to tell you any of this. It's not what I wanted to do. He was convicted of murdering Stanislav the clown.'

'In which prison in Scotland?' I asked.

'There are only a few. Open prisons that is, which is where they send tail-enders,' said this Andrew bloke. 'It shouldn't be hard to find out.'

'Thanks, Hervie, like really thanks for everything,' I said.

'You're leaving?' he asked.

'I think I'll try Scotland,' I said.

eight

McCleod handed me a shotgun and the cartridges that went with it and showed me how to load it.

There was a little platform he had erected in a tree from which you could look down on the entire sloping hillside where the sheep grazed. A ladder led up to the platform, which was like a raft made of logs lashed together, along with a tarpaulin above that gave shelter against the rain. It stayed quite dry, and I reckoned it would unless there was a storm.

McCleod had thought of everything to equip the little shelter. He had pillows and two pairs of binoculars. The shotgun had no telescope fitted to it, but he showed me how to line up the blob in the little notched V on the sight. I used to practise taking aim without firing the damned thing at first.

'Ever used one of these before?'

'Yes,' I said, 'with my dad, we used to go shooting in the jungles in Bangladesh.' It was rubbish, of course.

'Jungles in Bangladesh,' he said, looking in my face as though I was mad.

The hut, my hut, an actual little house, was a hundred yards away. He called it the cabin. It was my home. It had a bed and a telly and a cooking range with a gas cylinder and a sink but no taps. I had to get the water from a rubber pipe that came in through the window and was connected to a pump at the side of the cattle shed.

A hundred yards further down the slope was McCleod's house. He lived there alone, except when he was up in the cabin or mooching around on the farm with his tractor or other equipment. But now he'd hired me he didn't need to be on the platform at all.

All the time I was thinking of Hervie and what they'd do to him. The copper who'd brought me in asked me where I could be contacted if the trial went ahead and they needed me for evidence, so I gave Das's address in Slough, because they wouldn't let me go without giving some address. Then I walked to the roundabout where I could catch a ride.

I felt guilty. Had I grassed up old Hervie? I said I heard Anson shouting. Would that put Hervie behind bars? Straight up, I knew a lot of goonish kids who said anything and thought worse. They could get a person in trouble if they wanted. Was Anson one of them? Or had Hervie really gone for him and touched him up in the dark. They seemed to be good friends. I said all this to the inspector. And now I felt bad, guilty.

On the high road, I had hitched a ride with a German truck driver who talked about nothing but what he had seen on a safari in Africa. He said he saw lions and gorillas and mad dogs and elephants. I said I'd seen them in the zoo. He said it was not the same.

He dropped me at a place called Crewe.

I went to the station and got a train to Scotland. I asked an old lady where she was going and she said Dundee and she asked me where I was going and I said I was going to Dundee too. She said we had to change twice and she shared her sandwiches with me and we drank coffee out of her thermos. The trip took nearly a whole day and the old lady said that slow trains were cheaper. She let me know when the next stop was Dundee.

There was no way I could find out what happened to Hervie. I felt rotten about him, because the copper took some of what I said down, come to think of it. At least I hadn't signed anything. They hadn't made me sign, so I didn't think they could use it in court, but they'd still get him.

They were a bit sneaky, saying they were taking him in for his own protection and then when he went, turning it against him. And asking me questions to see if there was any fire where there had been some smoke from Anson.

Still, I was on the road to Scotland.

'I one Rashid Rashid am dead. Dead and yet alive.'

My heart ached for my mum now. I mean that for real. Verbatim. Every time I thought of her I got a little stab in my chest. But there was nothing I could do. I could see the cops stashing all the cards she'd been sending and intercepting all the phone calls she probably made and waiting for her or tracing her back to wherever she was.

Maybe she'd even come back and was looking for me and had put out the alert, because this was a fair country, even if the drama teacher said it wasn't – but never mind about her, I guess she wanted to feel that she was living amongst people who were filled with hate and that, just so she could feel a bit of a heroine and on the right side and everything.

I felt that they wouldn't actually get my mum in the end. They'd know that the guys with the false passport gear and the connections with Paris and Belgium had just moved in on me without my inviting them. The only problem might be that her name was Rabinovitch and she wouldn't be able to say where my dad was, which might seem suspicious. But still it was a free country and she could easily reply, 'None of your business.'

So I asked the old lady if there were any prisons she knew of.

'Oh aye,' she says. 'There are a lot of prisons in Scotland.'

She knew there was one near Dundee. You could

209

get to it from the next station.

'Is it open?'

'Open and shut,' she said.

I got off at the little station and began walking. That was where McCleod found me – walking down the road – and he asked me if I wanted a job looking after sheep.

I said that was just what I was looking for. I didn't want to tell him I was looking to visit the prison. I'd find a base and then move from there. He had stopped his van and he asked me to hop in.

'Shepherds are difficult to find. They push off to Dundee these lads, and Glasgow, and never come back. You didn't see a mob on the train did you?'

'Fans? There were no fans on the train. There was almost nobody.'

He nodded. 'I watch out on the roads for them. They'll come by road, rail, maybe helicopter. One never knows.'

I didn't know what he was talking about.

McCleod said he had a farm and needed someone to ward off the wild dogs. He'd pay and I'd get food and shelter.

'If you're wandering around Kildrummy, you must have come looking for a job,' he said. 'I'd do it myself but it needs to be dawn to dusk. I'll give you some relief. And the nights are yours but it's early rising on the farm.'

It was early rising. By five thirty McCleod would come with a torch and get me up. I'd make myself some coffee, climb the platform with my gun and go to sleep again.

'Mad dogs. They won't come at night,' he said.

The job was simple. He was convinced that there was a pack of sheep dogs that had gone mad and had left the outlying farms of the district. They had got together and formed a pack, all mad, all infected with some wolfish lust. They were living rough and eating sheep and their leader was blind. He believed it.

'They'll scatter if you shoot,' he said. 'They won't hold their ground. They are thieves and they live in the caves in the hills and prowl the farms. They've turned into wolves. Blind as a bat, but keen of ear, their leader . . .'

He said other farmers had lost sheep. This stuff made me nervous. Suppose the mad dogs came through the window of the cabin at night while I was in bed and attacked me?

'What would they want with a black boy,' he laughed. 'They're after food, mon. They eat sheep's guts, not black boys. You shoot on sight.'

'Have you seen them?'

He looked at me as though I was accusing him of being off his head, which I was.

'Seen them? Ay. When they get blood and wool off an animal on their mouths, it looks like they're frothing and foaming, but don't you mind that. Shoot to kill, mon.'

In the next few days I asked permission to practise my shooting on tin cans. I stacked them in a pyramid and shot. The gun was none too particular. If you shot at one it blew ten cans away.

I sat all day, day after day on the raft in the tree. McCleod gave me books and said reading was permitted. I never read so much stuff in my life. He had no good books, though. Only Dickens and a book called *How to Win Friends and Influence People* and since there was no one to make friends with around, I left that one alone. I just took a story of Dickens which was quite thick and I had my dictionary and thesaurus so no book could scare me at all. I didn't get put off.

At night the wind would start making weird sounds through the grass and round the mountains and I had to stop it coming through the cracks under the door and by the window frame. I cut bits of blanket and nailed them down to stop up the gaps, like carpet.

McCleod would come at night before he slept and say he'd come to see if everything was all right with me and whether I'd seen anything that day. I never saw nothing, but McCleod was not really there to enquire. He wanted to talk to me, to anyone. He'd stay an hour or more before going back to his croft with the heavy torch.

'I want a day or two off,' I said after a week. I didn't

want to say it was to visit a prison.

'I can't afford that,' said McCleod. 'They'll strike any time.'

He told me he was a scientist. He'd got rid of one kind of sheep-tick from his entire flock and then other farmers heard of what he used for dips and they followed him. He was known all over the country, he said. He'd won prizes at the fairs for the stuff he made.

'You're a black fellow, aren't you? You told me yourself, Bangladesh,' he said on the second night he stopped by.

'Yes, I am,' I agreed.

'Well, there's people starving out there,' he said. 'As far as sheep are concerned, I know that I'm growing food and I'm growing wool and that's helpful. To someone. And do you see what I am doing to help?'

I didn't know what he meant.

He got to coming every day just to talk. We would talk about the bit of the story I had read from *The Tale Of Two Cities* that day and it was funny how McCleod remembered the lot. He would chuckle at some little bit of a description he remembered from that part of the book. He was good on memory.

One day he said, 'We are good friends. I can tell you the secret of the grass.'

I had come to expect some crazy things from McCleod. He would talk about the mad dogs and the blind one that led them, and after two weeks or more of seeing nothing of these dogs, I began to doubt their existence. Maybe McCleod just wanted someone to talk to at nights after dinner. He must have known there were no mad dogs that came in packs by day. It was in his dreams.

I hadn't seen anyone else except the postman in a post van, for days, and there was the man who cleaned the sheep pen and did the jobs. I had things to cook for myself and McCleod would fetch vegetables and bread and milk. His own produce, he said and from the weight of it, certainly his own bread.

But the secret of the grass. I wanted the secret and so I reminded him the next day, that he had not yet revealed it.

'Yes, I know. But this, this is top secret,' he said. 'That grass you're watching over. It's very special grass. Very special indeed. It has been grown in Mexico and scientifically designed to strengthen the sheep against a particular virus. They eat the grass and become extra strong to beat something like our chicken pox, you know. The food gets rid of the pox for ever. A miracle. Scientific research, laddie.'

'That's good,' I said.

'But you're not to tell anyone,' said McCleod. 'It's the Ministry handles it, so we must keep it a secret. They come round to test my sheep. When the new ewes come, they'll be free of the pox.'

I found that the name of the prison was Noranside and it was near a small place called Forfar. I phoned it and it was true. They did have a prisoner called Joshua Rabinovitch. I told the woman on the end of the phone that he didn't know me but I wanted to visit him. She said he'd have to sign a visiting order, but I could write to him if I wanted.

By night I wrote to him and sent the letter off.

Dear Joshua Rabinovitch,

I am sure I am your grandson, because I am the son of Esther, your daughter. She is not in Britain at present. She never told me much about you but it is important that I find you.

I tracked you down through circus posters.

I am fourteen years old and would like to meet you.

Thank you. I have written my address above and would like you to agree to see me.

Your grandson,

Rashid Rashid

p.s. Don't be put off by the name. This is genuine and I can explain who I am and everything.

Maybe he'd get back to me. I would hang on and earn some money whether I saw him or not, and if I earned six weeks money there, I could get back to London maybe and look for mum. The thought haunted me

215

that maybe she was back.

McCleod didn't know this, but what had happened to everyone I'd met, the mad mullah, Das, Alice and Hervie was that they had been taken away. I couldn't say where they'd been taken, but I was sure I'd brought them bad luck. And it must have been just luck because nothing I had done got them into trouble. I was clear of that.

McCleod couldn't get in trouble. There was nothing for him to get in trouble about. He paid me good money and got me my food and everything, even toothpaste, and I never had to buy anything.

After ten days I got a letter in the post. It was the letter I had sent. There was a typewritten note attached to it.

From Noranside open prison
This letter has been returned to the sender because the prisoner to whom it was addressed refuses to accept it.

At least I knew he was there. So I wrote another letter:

Dear Joshua Rabinovitch,
You refused my first letter. This is your grandson and I'm fourteen years old, man, and I don't have no one but you. That's why I've tracked you down. Mum's gone away working somewhere else and I've got into lots of trouble

216

with the law and people.

I got the statue of Stanislav from Mum, and then in my investigations someone told me that he was murdered. I am very sorry because I knew he was your friend.

I can't force you to see me, but I've come all the way here and am working as a security guard on a Scottish farm just because of you.

You may be in trouble, but I am willing to believe your side of the story.
Your grandson,
Rashid Rashid

I sent it and the old letter with it.

For weeks there was no reply. I waited for the post every day.

While I stayed there, sitting on the raft in the tree, reading *A Tale of Two Cities* and then *Great Expectations* and after that, half of *The Old Curiosity Shop*. I never had to spend anything and I never saw a mad dog even though McCleod said on two mornings that he had heard them howling from their cave in the night.

I asked him why the Council didn't go out and find them in the cave if they were dangerous and mad and then shoot them or give them a lethal injection.

'They don't want to make the whole thing public because then reporters would turn up and the photographers and the tourists wouldn't come to Scotland if there were mad dogs about. What's more, the stupid

English would get one of these food scares and wouldn't buy our wool or lamb.'

'I think you and the other farmers should form a posse like they do in the western films and go out and hunt them down if they are dangerous.'

McCleod thought for a while and then he said he didn't get on with his neighbours. They were old-fashioned and ignorant and he couldn't talk to them. I didn't know if any of this was true, but it wasn't my business.

I couldn't figure him out in fact. He seemed happy to be alone on the farm, but he was still lonely. He never asked me to go and eat supper with him. I always had bread and cheese and cans of spaghetti which I could open for supper so it was OK but he always preferred to come to my cabin instead of inviting me to the farmhouse. It may be that he thought I was just one of the workers, though he didn't seem to have many more. There was one boy who was a bit slow. I saw him from a distance tipping cans of chemicals into the sheep bath. I tried to talk to him once but he didn't look like he understood me.

I had been into McCleod's farmhouse once and he did tell me that he was married but he never mentioned any children and didn't say what happened to his wife. I had gone for more gun cartridges and he was very hospitable. He gave me some beer, and in his kitchen I saw the photograph of the wife and a girl.

'Is that your family?' I asked.

'The one girl, yes,' he said. 'Sent her to university. We don't see eye to eye.'

One day wandering down the hillside, I found a grave with a wooden cross to mark it. The grass had grown over it so there wasn't any sign of a bump in the land, but it could have been his wife's grave or that of his favourite sheep. I reckoned that the sheep couldn't have been a Christian and wouldn't have needed a big cross made of logs.

I never asked him about it.

Then the letter came from Granddad.

My Dear Rashid,

Yes, come and see me. I am worried to hear that our Esther is not with you and that you don't know her whereabouts, but I shall send you a form after this date for you to fill in because that's what the authorities require. I never even knew I had a grandson. But you are the only one. Do come here, but understand, please, why I am here and what I did and did not do.

Your grandfather,

Josh

I cried. I read it ten times and I cried again.

In the mornings the sun would appear suddenly over the hillside and pour light straight into the window of my cabin. I didn't draw the little curtain because I'd got used to waking up on my own before McCleod came by with his whistling and his good mornings. So early one morning I was startled awake by him rushing up to the cabin. I used to lock the door in case the mad dogs ventured. McCleod banged at the door.

'They're here,' he said, as I opened it. 'Come on.'

He rushed in, grabbed the gun from its rack on the wall and dashed out again. I dragged my jeans on and ran after him. It wasn't quite light yet, the night was just lifting and I could only see a little way across the field. I thought McCleod meant the dogs had come and I didn't feel brave.

'Shall we go up to the raft and wait?' I asked.

'They're not here; over the hill,' he said.

We went down the path next to the sheep pasture. McCleod was running. As we rounded the shoulder of the hill I saw what he meant. There were about a hundred people and three tractors and they were digging up part of the hillside. They must have come off the road below and onto McCleod's land. He was very agitated.

As we got closer I saw that alongside the bunch of people carrying spades there were TV cameras and photographers. They had parked their cars along the side road that led to the farm, and they must have smashed through the wooden barriers to get the tractors in.

'What do you think you're doing?' McCleod shouted.

The people had a leader, a bald geezer about the same shape and size as McCleod.

'What do you think we're doing?' he mocked.

'Get off my land, you're trespassing.' McCleod was shaking with anger.

'We are acting for the people of Scotland,' said the bald bloke.

There were men and women behind the leader and they began to shout at McCleod.

'You are playing with our lives,' one was saying.

I got it then. They were protesters come against McCleod for his Ministry experiment. The secret of the grass was out.

I was standing behind him and I noticed that McCleod seemed to be looking for someone in the group of protesters. This is what he had been waiting for. He saw her.

'I thought you'd fetch them one day to ruin me,' he shouted. He pointed at a girl in the middle of the group. 'That's my daughter you've got there. You know that, you bastards. You're back are you, Clare?'

His daughter pushed her way forward.

'I warned you, Dad. We can't allow you to destroy the planet.'

Now McCleod lost it completely.

'Get off my land, all of you. Now. You too, Clare. I

don't care for your hooligans. Take them and go. I've had enough grief from you. Go. Or I'll shoot. Get those machines off my farm. I'll have you.'

He was furious. He gave me the gun to hold, went up to the leader and grabbed him by the collar. The bald bloke staggered, putting out his hands, and I realised he was blind. McCleod was about to punch him when five women, including Clare, grabbed McCleod, threw him down in the mud and sat on him. McCleod was screaming all sorts of abuse at them and the photographers and TV crew were furiously taking pictures.

McCleod fought the women off. He was spitting angry now. He ran towards me and grabbed the gun.

'Tell them to get the tractors off my farm,' he shouted.

The leader took no notice. The people started shouting. 'No GM crops in Scotland. Save our nature, save our land.'

'Bastards.' McCleod lifted the gun to his shoulder and, before I could stop him, he aimed at the tractors which were merrily digging up his seeds. He pulled the trigger. He must have hit one of the tractor drivers because a man fell out of the cab onto the mud. The tractor went on by itself for a while and then stopped. The people all rushed to see if the driver was badly hurt.

McCleod was stunned by what he had done. He let

the gun fall to the ground. He wasn't fighting now.

Someone shouted, 'Get some bandages.'

Judging by the shouts of his friends I figured that the man was not dead, just hurt, probably shot in the side with the round pellets. Clare came up to her father. She was hysterical.

'What have you done? Look what you've done,' she screamed.

'And you, haven't you done enough to your own father and to the memory of your mother?' McCleod shouted.

'Don't you mention her,' hissed his daughter. 'You killed her with the poisons you use, you vandal. I'm ashamed to call you my father. I want to tear your whole farm apart!'

McCleod stood there and took it. He must have known about his daughter, her hatred of him. But he was shattered by it. He stood still like a scarecrow with the mud all over him.

I realised that this was what he had been afraid of. These were the mad dogs he was talking about, with their leader being blind.

The police had arrived in force by now, along with the ambulance.

'Do you work here?' one of the protest people asked me.

I didn't owe him an answer so I just ran off.

It was daylight when I got to the cabin, but it was

too early for the postman. I was waiting for the letter telling me the date on which I could visit the prison, but it hadn't arrived. My grandfather had said he wanted to see me and now the chance was slipping away.

I took the money I had saved and put my clothes in a plastic bag. Then I started down to the small road on the other side of the hill.

I heard the voices of the protesters and more cars turning up. Probably the police were taking McCleod away for attempted murder or something. I never got to thank him or to say goodbye.

nine

Iwas going to Noranside Prison, to see Joshua Rabbit.

I'd started looking for him because he could tell me where my mother's birth certificate was. But as I went on the bus from Forfar to Noranside, I'd forgotten this. I just wanted to see him because he was my grandfather. I had his letter and I looked at it over and over.

The bus dropped me in the village and I was given directions to the prison. It was a fair walk from the road, but it wasn't all walls and barbed wire as I expected. It was like a college or something, and I walked up to the lodge and said I'd like to see my grandfather.

They asked me if I had a date on a visiting order and I said I only had a letter saying that he wanted to see me.

The geezer at the lodge told me to wait outside. About half-an-hour later a lady came up to me and asked me what I wanted and I told her all over again. She was not wearing a uniform. She looked like a smart dinner lady from school.

The lady said a visit would be OK, but I should wait an hour or come back in the afternoon. I told her the truth. I said I'd hang about.

After an hour they took me into the prison. They put me in a room and they brought Joshua Rabinovitch to see me.

I swear he looked like Mum. The eyes and the smile. He was a big geezer, with a paunch and a nearly bald head and everything and Mum is very thin and has very beautiful hair, but she was his daughter, you could see it straightaway.

'Rashid?' he says.

'Yeah,' I say.

He grabs me by both shoulders and looks in my eyes. And I look in his eyes and I don't know what he's going to do, but his eyes start watering. He's crying.

'Why did you want to find me?' he asks.

'Because my mum is out of the country and I got into a bit of trouble. My other granddad, you know, my dad's father. He came and lived with us and then he died.'

'Who is your dad?' he asks

I shake my head.

'And where is my Esther? You know we don't talk.'

'I know that much,' I say, 'but I don't know why.'

Then he grabs two armchairs and sits next to me and holds both my hands.

'Because she thinks I killed Stanislav, who was her mother's husband. Do you get it?'

'The clown?'

'Yes. He was my friend. He had a wife but he was very cruel to her and she and I fell in love. We went away together to build a new life for ourselves, and we had a daughter, your mother. But Stanislav followed us.'

'And you killed him?'

'No. I think he killed himself. But no one believed me. Not even my own daughter.'

'I believe you,' I said.

He laughed.

'Why do you believe me?'

'I don't think you killed anybody.'

'Stanislav was my greatest friend but he was a bit crazy. He was cruel to his wife and he drove her away. He was a genius, but he was depressed, sad. He knew about poisons. He ate poison flowers and died.'

'Why?'

'Who can say? Maybe because I had taken his wife away. Maybe because in all those years he didn't have children with her. Maybe because he couldn't go on any more. But I didn't kill him. Now, tell me how you found me.'

He hugged me. We talked for two hours. The next day I came back again and we walked in the gardens and talked some more. He said he would be in prison for another two years but he wanted to see my mother when I found her. I said that's what I was going to do.

The boss of the prison gave me a piece of paper which said that Josh was my grandfather. It was what they called an affidavit and he said I could use it to prove whose grandson I was at least.

Josh and I decided that the best way to get news of my mum would be to go to London and try and track down Sophie, my mum's dancing mate. She used to go abroad too for dancing, but at least her flat would not have been taken over by aliens so there would be someone there even if she was not and they could maybe tell me about Mum.

I was fed up of hitching and truck drivers and maniacs who saw mad dogs, so I actually bought a ticket and came down to London by coach. I got to Sophie's house but there was no one there. I waited a day and a night. Maybe she'd return. She didn't. She'd left it locked up.

I thought about my options. I could go to my flat and see what had happened there or go back to my school and let them hand me over to the Social. No insult, but it was the last thing I wanted to do.

I still had the keys to Das's place in Slough. Maybe he was back and I could use that as a base and then think of my next step. I wanted to find a normal life. I wanted to find my mum and what was funny is that Das, who was not really normal was the person I thought would help me best. I reckoned I could tell Das everything. Hervie, McCleod, the squatters in my flat, everything, and he wouldn't grass me and he wouldn't be shocked.

'I, one Fabio Romani . . . ' It was time for Fabio to come out of the land of the dead and face it, whatever it was.

I turned the key and the door opened. There was someone living there. I could hear music. So Das was back and that made my heart beat faster. That was lucky.

'Dr Bronco,' I shouted, but the person who came out on to the landing was not Das. Still, it was someone I recognised. It was the bloke Alice had met in the Leicester shopping mall. The bloke she said was a plainclothes copper. The bloke who looked like an Italian hip-hop star.

'What are you doing in my house?' he said. He looked as if he was going to charge down the stairs and hit me.

'I thought it was Das's house. He gave me a key.'

A woman wearing a dressing gown came out of the room. It was Alice.

'Rashid! It's OK, Zeb, this is Rashid. Where did you come from? Where have you been?'

'I thought you were on the run,' I said.

'I'll explain it all,' she said. 'I'm sorry.'

But she didn't have to explain. I knew it straight off.

229

She had told me lies. The man Sebastian, Zeb, had come back, found us in Leicester and she had gone back with him. She had made up the story about him being a bent plainclothes cop come to warn her. It was crap. She just got fed up of what she was doing and wanted to go back to her old ways with this bloke.

'Don't bother, I get it,' I said.

'You can stay,' she added.

'So where's Das?'

'He's away. They put him away. Not for drugs, for stabbing someone. But he'll be out in a few months.'

'And where are the other girls? I suppose you're all back together, you and Rag, Tag and Bobtail?'

'Who is this kid?' Zeb asked.

Alice ignored him. 'Yes, all the girls are here. We're in business again. But Rashid, has your mum come back?'

I said no, and she said the first thing we had to do was find her.

'Come on Mad Hatter, it's Alice. You can forgive Alice.'

'Forgive? You never done me nothing. You just told me lies.'

'Not lies,' she said later, after I'd been given tea and egg and chips. 'I was just beaten. I don't think you know how exhausted I got, keeping up the pretence. It's not easy getting away from who you are. We couldn't get away from the past could we?'

I was thinking she should speak for herself.

'So you just take me to a strange town and walk out, yeah?'

'I'm really sorry, Rashid, but I had to grab on to something even if it was dusty old Zeb and his games and his lies and his rackets. You're lucky . . . '

'Me, lucky?'

'At least your mum's nice. When she comes back you'll have someone who loves you.'

'Don't talk wet. She's not coming back now, is she?'

'I think she is. She's much more human than me, from what you've told me and she'll be missing you desperately and that's all she'll be thinking of. But Rashid . . . I'm sorry I couldn't hang about, that it ended like that.'

'I didn't really know you anyway,' I shrugged.

'Don't say that!' she said. A look of pain came over her face and then I regretted saying it.

'You know the money I got and you thought I was selling myself? I wasn't. I called the old numbers I had. The lonely hearts guys and said I needed money. They gave it to me. The old geezer you saw in the pub? I called him and he came from Birmingham to give me money. Amazing.'

That part I hadn't worked out and I didn't know what to say. I told her I'd found Josh.

'He's alive? Where is he.' She genuinely wanted to know so I told her.

'He's innocent,' I said. 'And he's been more than twenty years inside.'

'Now find your mum,' said Alice.

As we were talking, the girls came back. Rag, Tag and Bobtail were not their real names, but that's what they called themselves on the computer and they were getting on with it and taking people's cash.

'I thought you were never going to do that again,' I said to Daffy. 'What happened to Alice?'

She didn't reply but just smiled.

Zeb wasn't as bad as I thought he was. In the next two days he tried to get me to see Das in prison but they wouldn't let me in because there was some law about being underage and not related to the prisoner. I wrote him a letter instead. Zeb went and visited Das regularly. It was nice of him.

But things don't last. I stayed there two days and then they came for me, the Social and Kristina, and they said if I didn't go with them they'd have the police round. Zeb said I should go even though Alice made a fuss and started crying. They'd come from London to track me down. I went with them.

I had the letter from Joshua's place and I showed it to them.

'I'm not a nowhere person any more. That's my grandfather and he's British and he's a guest of the queen at present,' I said.

Kristina was impressed. She took me back to the

232

care hostel and I told her that there was no way I'd stay. I had my papers now. She agreed because she's decent but the cops got involved and wanted me for all sorts of questioning. I was wondering why they hadn't put Interpol on the case. There was Herv the Perv and there were the guys who'd taken my flat and their immigration business and then there was Frankie to whom I'd done damage.

For all these reasons, they said they had to check me out and so they brought me here. I said it was jail where I was writing the whole story down, but it ain't really. It's a detention centre and they put people who don't have papers here. Kristina said it's better than going with the police.

Zeb is taking my papers, the affidavit and everything to his friend at the Law Centre to get me out. I can't leave until they've finished with me and are sure of who I am and what they should do with me. I asked for a copy of *The Old Curiosity Shop*, because I wanted to know how the story ends. You can't just leave a story like that. So I've been reading it, a new copy.

And then this; writing this down for Kristina. It's the worst thing I've experienced in all my time on the run because they've really got me just sitting here writing on their computer. Zeb and Alice have been round to see me and Zeb said he's been to Sophie's address and nosed about and she's coming home next week.

ten

OK, stop press. Zeb's found Mum. Just like that. He's come round and told Kristina that he can now locate her. He brought an order from some court or something and Kristina started jumping for joy and kissing me as though she had done it. Then ten people signed papers and they let me out.

Zeb took me in his car and we went to London and back to Sophie's flat. The neighbours had told him that she still lived there and was coming back from some place in the next week.

That's why we were there. I don't know what Zeb did to convince them to let me out but it felt good to be free.

So now I'm writing this just to finish off the story, but not on the detention computer. I won't tell you where I'm writing from because that gives the game away, so you'll have to read on if you've got this far.

Sophie couldn't believe her eyes. She fell upon me as though I was her son.

'Rashid, my God, your mother's been looking for

you for months. She's desperate. She rushed back when the phone got cut off and all that stuff about the people moving into your flat. How did all that happen? And we were worried sick and the police are looking for you . . . '

'Where is she?'

'She'll be right here. You're not going anywhere,' Sophie said, and she got on the phone.

Mum was out in Devon talking to the police who'd last seen me with Hervie. They knew it was me by now.

Sophie passed me the phone.

'Hello, darling! Thank God. Oh, thank God,' she said. And she sounded strange. She was actually blubbing, crying, man.

'Hi Mum,' I said. I didn't know what else to say.

'Don't you want to see me?'

'Course I do,' I said. 'I found Granddad. Your father.'

She was quiet on the phone for a bit then she says, 'Yes, we'll talk about that.' And then she says not to go an inch away, to wait just there because she was driving back right then and if she could fly she would and where had I been to find Granddad and how she had tried a thousand times to find me and I just said, 'You just come, Mum, OK? Catch up with you later.'

I put the phone down but she wouldn't go, she rang again and she said she just wanted to hear my voice and she wanted Sophie to say what I looked like and again for me to say something, anything to her. She rang six times like she was crazy or something.

I got a bit fed up of it so I told Sophie I'd go back with Zeb and fetch my gear from Slough.

'Oh no you're not. I'm not letting you out of my sight,' Sophie said.

'I've got my savings there,' I said. 'Where are we going to live?'

'I don't think your savings are going to matter. Or your flat. Your mum's talked to Scotland Yard and they know that you moved out before the gang moved in. You won't need the flat anyway.'

'Are we staying with you?'

'No, I'll let your mother tell you herself.'

'Happy endings,' Zeb said. Then he turned to Sophie. 'Rashid tells me you're a dancer.'

'Yeah. But I'm fed up of it. Too much travelling.'

'Can you use a computer? Be an actress, make up letters? Do you like meeting people?'

'No she can't and she doesn't,' I said.

'Those are all the things I'm good at,' Sophie said. They were getting on good.

'Junior is sweet on my girl,' Zeb said.

I think I was blushing. Whatever the truth of it was, he shouldn't have said it.

'But I don't mind sharing her with my friend Rashid,' he added.

'I'll see you later Zeb. I'll wait for Mum. Thanks. And tell them all thanks and I'll be round, right?'

Over the next few hours Sophie kept telling me how they had looked all over Britain for me. Then a Jag drew up and we saw it from the window. Mum got out. She was wearing a very fancy outfit, white trousers and a long white coat thing on top.

Mum rushed in and grabbed me and just held on to me for minutes and started to cry. And then the fellow who'd been driving her came in. He was a tall bloke with dark hair and sharp features. Quite handsome I suppose.

When Mum finally stopped hugging me and dried her eyes, she introduced me to him. He was just standing patiently and waiting for us to finish and I could see him over her shoulders. He was smiling at me uncertainly, wondering whether to smile outright and give me a big cheesy one or to wait.

'My Rashid,' she said. 'This is Nafeez.'

He was Egyptian but he lived in Paris and he made movies in America and he and Mum were going to buy a house in London and get married, but only when they had found me.

He was quite frank. He said he was very glad they'd found me because now Gypsy would marry him and everything swung on whether I was safe. And I was.

Some kids would be jealous of a feller who wanted to marry their Mum, but I wasn't. He looked decent and he was rich and he looked like he loved my mum and that's good and she looked at him special, like he'd saved her and that was wet, wet, wet, but I wasn't placed to interfere.

I moved into the room above theirs in a very posh hotel in London and in four days they'd bought a grand house. Nafeez was trying to be good to me, but not in a smarmy way. He began talking about where I could go to college and that. I hadn't even got back to school and he was talking about which universities in America were any good.

She told me all about how she'd been worried about me and asked me for every detail of everything I'd done. I didn't tell her the lot. There are some things that adults get shocked by, things they can't take.

She wanted to marry Nafeez and kept asking me if it was OK with me.

I said I wasn't bothered, she could marry whoever she liked.

I was thinking about Hervie and about the mad fellow McCleod. I asked Das to find out where they were and he said he would. He did. Hervie had been held for six months before his trial came up and then the cops said they had nothing against him so they let him go. His old house in the village had been sold so he couldn't go back, but I'm thinking of going back there and asking the vicar to tell me where old Hervie has got to and maybe visit him.

And McCleod, he was in court too for shooting someone, but some American company what owns the seeds he was planting got him off and they gave him big money too. If I go up to see granddad, there's another visit I've got to do, but maybe mum won't get on with him.

Then they said I had to go to a new school but I said I wanted to get back to my old one and that led to an argument and I shouted at mum. Nafeez settled the argument. I could try the school here and if I found it too snobby he'd send me down to Hackney every day, even if he had to get a car and chauffeur to drive me. As if! But the same day my mum went and equipped my room in the new house and Nafeez went and got me a computer because I'd said I had been using one in the job I was doing in Leicester.

I turned on the computer.

Dear Alice,

I once told you that I wondered why a netted box holding rabbits was called a 'Run' when in fact it stopped them running? I've been in the same place now for some weeks and I'm beginning to like it. Run means your own patch. I suppose I was a bit slow in catching on. Write to me.
Yours still,
The Mad Hatter

That evening there was an answer.

Dear Mad Hatter,

*Let's see . . . mmm . . . 'Rabbits', 'Slow in catching on' –
a Run? Is it about a race? – Got it! The Hare and Tortoise.
But in which town?*

*Of course we should write to each other. I got a letter
from Bronco Das. He says he's out in a few weeks. Will
your mum and your new dad let you see a jailbird?*

*I'm writing this from – guess where? India. Thinking of
you. Zeb and I pulled up our roots and decided to find out
what the world was like. Now I'm on the run and I love it.*

*I don't want to get serious or sentimental but I must say
it once. Please believe me, I did love you, and I thought you
were interesting and fanciable even, but then you were so
young, too young and I had to get away from that. 'Can't
have everything' is what living teaches you.*

*I suppose the next time I see you, you'll be talking with a
posh accent from your new school and be a different person
with a newish life, but don't forget . . .*
Your
Alice